❧The Sorority❧
MERILYNN

Books by Tamara Thorne

HAUNTED

MOONFALL

ETERNITY

CANDLE BAY

BAD THINGS

THE FORGOTTEN

The Sorority Trilogy
EVE
MERILYNN

⊰THE SORORITY⊱
MERILYNN

TAMARA THORNE

PINNACLE BOOKS
Kensington Publishing Corp.

PINNACLE BOOKS are published by

Kensington Publishing Corp.
850 Third Avenue
New York, NY 10022

Pinnacle and the P logo Reg. U.S. Pat. & TM Off.

ISBN 0-7394-3709-7

Printed in the United States of America

For Q.L. Pearce
Purveyor of magical mystery tours
Thanks for all the rides
Past, present, and future.

Applehead Lake
Cheerleading Camp

Eight Years Ago

One

"A long time ago, the town of Applehead was located right there under the lake." Counselor Allie Mayhew pointed toward the lake, its black water slowly rippling with silver moonlight.

Merilynn Morris, sitting on a log across the crackling campfire from Allie, shivered with delight and anticipation, then glanced at the other campers gathered on the circle of logs. Most of the preteen girls were saucer-eyed with pleasurable terror, though a few, like Eve Camlan, looked honestly afraid. And then there was Sam Penrose, beside Merilynn. Sam looked—well, she looked bored.

But Merilynn knew that was just a facade, Sam's usual nothing-bothers-me attitude. After yesterday's trip to the island, how could it be anything else? She hadn't been able to talk to Sam or Eve today, to find out what they were really thinking about the previous day's adventures, but she didn't have to be a genius to know that both of them were avoiding her. They didn't want to talk about it. *Chickens!*

"Everyone knew the town was going to be flooded," Allie Mayhew went on. "And even though most people were a little sorry about losing their orchards and their old homes, they understood that their valley was the only logical place for a reservoir and that because of the drought that had plagued them for four years already, their trees would die of thirst anyway.

"So they moved, leaving their homes and apple trees behind. Many left and helped found the little village of Crackle Hill—"

"That's Caledonia now," some camper blurted.

"That's right, Megan," Allie said, nodding. "Others went farther north or south, but the people who really loved the valley and this forest, they stayed right here."

"Right here?" Merilynn asked. *Get to the ghost stories already!*

"Yes, some did. The main house where we have our meals and indoor meetings here at camp once belonged to a family named Gayle. Mr. and Mrs. Gayle had just one daughter and after she died, they moved away and willed the property to Greenbriar University."

"How did Holly Gayle die?" Merilynn prompted.

"You're a glutton for ghost stories, Merilynn," Allie said, smiling. "We've already told the story of Holly. She drowned."

"You've only told it twice." Merilynn looked around for support from her fellow campers. "Have *you* ever seen her ghost?"

Girls murmured, titillated.

"Me?" Allie asked.

Merilynn nodded.

Everyone stared at the counselor, who looked around, as if checking to make sure no one else was listening. Many of the girls turned their heads, too, nervously, probably more worried about Holly's ghost than eavesdropping counselors. In absolute heaven, Merilynn asked, "Have you, Allie? Have *you* seen her?"

"Well . . . maybe."

Hushed gasps hissed through the air. The firelight wavered.

"No," Allie added. "I can't really say I saw her. I just imagined it, I'm sure."

"Oh, come on, Allie," Merilynn urged. "Tell us anyway."

"Well . . ." She looked at the girls appraisingly. "It was last summer."

Tell! Tell! Tell! Merilynn could barely sit still.

"It was early September, the day after the last campers left for home. Only we—the counselors— were still here, cleaning up and closing things up for the season. That last night, we had the guys—the counselors from the football camp across the lake,"—she pointed—"over for our annual party. They drove over. It was still light out, only about six o'clock, when they arrived, but you know how these woods are. It seemed dark."

Allie paused dramatically, then glanced at her wristwatch. "It's late. Maybe I should finish the story tomorrow night—"

Girls moaned and begged, which Merilynn knew was just what she wanted. Allie was her favorite counselor because she loved telling stories.

"Okay. There were nearly two dozen of us altogether, us and the guys. We had a barbecue and then we all sat right here and toasted marshmallows over the campfire."

"Did you drink?" Sam Penrose asked, doing her Spocky-eyebrow thing.

"Drink?" Allie asked. Then, shocked, "You mean alcohol?"

"Yes."

"Of course not! That's not allowed!"

Bull puckies, thought Merilynn, trying not to grin too much. She knew right where they hid the beer and wine coolers. So did Sam. They'd found the treasure trove together, hidden in an old hollow log. She launched an elbow into Sam's arm to keep her from saying so. It might be fun to see Allie's reaction, but it would ruin the ghost story.

Sam returned the poke so hard that Merilynn had to stifle a yelp. They exchanged a look. Merilynn knew the other girl wouldn't tell.

"So, what happened?" Sam asked. "Did someone pretend to be a ghost while you were toasting your marshmallows?"

Merilynn poked her again, glared at her. "Don't spoil this," she whispered.

Sam crossed her eyes at her, but nodded acquiescence.

"It wasn't while we were around the campfire," Allie said at last. "It was later. Down by the dock."

Everyone turned their heads toward the little dock poking out into the lake, rowboats leashed to it like puppy dogs. There was a small boathouse too, right up against the far side of the dock, but it was rarely used during camping season. At the moment, it was nothing but a dark smudge on the narrow beach.

"It was probably ten or eleven o'clock and we'd split up, you know, to walk around and talk. Hold hands."

A couple of more knowledgeable girls giggled. Allie Mayhew silenced them with silence.

"Nothing bad was going on," she said. Merilynn

knew she had to say that; then Sam leaned over and whispered, "Condoms" in her ear.

Merilynn just about lost it. To keep from laughing, she pinched the back of her hand until tears sprung into her eyes. She was going to have to get Sam back later. She was definitely messing with her.

"One of the guys and I were walking along the shore and we decided to go sit on the pier. We walked to the end, then sat down and took off our shoes so we could dangle our feet in the water."

Crickets chirped. Fire crackled.

"It was really dark. Darker than it is now. We were just talking and kind of looking down into the water. Way, way out, I saw a light come on under the water. One, then another."

Oohs and ahs, hushed, almost reverent, punctuated her pause.

"The other counselor saw them too. We looked at each other and he said, 'You know what that means?' and I said, 'What?'"

"What?" several girls murmured.

"He said the town was coming to life." Allie looked from girl to girl before adding, "'When the town starts coming to life,' he told me, 'that means Holly Gayle is taking a walk.'"

Merilynn saw Eve Camlan draw into herself, hugging herself with her arms. Merilynn felt sorry for her, being so afraid. But not that sorry. "And then you saw the ghost?" she asked Allie.

"Not yet. I got nervous. I mean, who wouldn't?"

Campers nodded enthusiastically.

"So I told Mark—the guy I was with—that we were just seeing starlight reflected on the water. He said maybe so.

"I stood up and said I was cold, you know, to get him to get off the dock." Flames glittered in Allie's wide eyes. "I mean, it was late, and those lights looked real, even if they weren't. I just couldn't stand having my feet in the water then, because I just *knew* one of Holly Gayle's cold, dead-white hands was going to reach out of the water and grab my ankle and pull me in!"

A lot of girls looked frightened now, but Merilynn leaned forward, enthralled. "What happened? What did you see?"

"Well, I pulled my sandals on and Mark got up. He teased me a little, but was pretty quick putting his own shoes back on. We turned around to walk back down the dock." Allie smiled for an instant, cut it off abruptly. "And then it happened. We saw *her.*"

Shocked inhalations, breaths held.

"And?" Merilynn said impatiently.

"She came out of the boathouse at the shoreline, right where we'd have to pass to get off the dock. For a minute, I thought she was just one of the other counselors. But she was wearing a long white dress. *Holly,* I thought. Mark stopped walking and just stared. Me too. And then I realized it was just one of the counselors pretending to be Holly to scare us. I mean, isn't that what you'd think?" She looked right at Merilynn.

"No," Merilynn said, throwing Allie off, loving that she could. *"I'd* think it was the ghost."

"Well, Merilynn," Allie said, fear actually showing in her eyes now, "you might have been right. It wasn't a counselor. The girl in white *seemed* to be walking— but too smoothly, like maybe she wasn't quite touching the ground. She was coming toward us, very slowly, but didn't seem to be walking on the dock exactly. I mean, really, she looked like she was *on the lake,* but that's impossible."

"If it was a ghost, it's not impossible," Merilynn said.

Girls giggled, clutching one another now.

"Well, Mark and I still thought it had to be a joke, so we just made ourselves head right toward her. You know, to get off the pier. As we approached the boathouse, though, the girl just vanished. Faded away into thin air. But before she was gone, I saw her face and hair. She was wet, her hair just hung around her face like she'd been in the lake. Her dress, too. I could see water dripping off her fingertips. And her face?"

Silence.

"It wasn't one of the counselors. I'd never seen her before. Her eyes seemed normal; then in the last second they seemed to be just dark smudges. Her face wasn't all there anymore."

Campers jabbered in soft tones, telling each other what they wanted to hear. Merilynn briefly caught Eve Camlan's gaze, saw the horror in her eyes, and sent her the gentlest smile she could muster. Then she rose and stretched, nonchalantly leaving the campfire circle to saunter—at least she hoped it looked like sauntering—twenty feet to the lake's edge.

The dark water rippled with silver moonlight. It was hard to be sure, but she thought she caught brief glimmers of deep golden light far out beneath the surface.

"Holly?" she whispered. "Holly, where are you?"

Two

"This isn't a very bright idea," Sam Penrose whispered to Merilynn after they successfully sneaked out of the little cabin full of sleeping girls. It was just past midnight as she rubbed sleep from her eyes, then bent to tie the laces on her Nikes. "I don't know why I let you talk me into this. We're really pushing our luck."

"We're fine, but hurry up," Merilynn whispered, drowning in impatience. "We have to get away from the cabins or they really will hear us and we'll be caught. And you know what that means!"

Sam stood up straight, zipped her windbreaker, and made a face. "Yeah. They'll make us practice cheers for a couple extra hours."

"Or expel us!" Merilynn suggested.

"Nah, they'd only do that if they found out about our trip to the island," Sam said. "Hmm. That wouldn't be a bad thing, would it? Not as bad as extra practice. God, this place is *so* stupid. I think I'd like to get expelled!"

Merilynn studied Sam's expression, but in the moonlight she couldn't quite decide if the girl was joking or serious. Joking, probably, but she couldn't take a chance. Though she didn't give a rat's butt about the cheering either, Merilynn sure as heck didn't want to get sent home early. "They can't find out about yesterday unless one of us tells them. And then they'd find out about Eve too, and she loves this place. We have to keep it a total secret for her sake."

"We wouldn't have to mention her." As she spoke, Sam started leading the way toward the boathouse, walking quietly, keeping to the shadows.

Merilynn followed, pleased. Despite all her griping, there was no way Sam Penrose could resist an adventure. "If you hate cheering, why'd you come to this camp?" she asked as soon as they were away from the cabins.

"To find out what makes girls want to be cheerleaders."

"What do you mean?"

Sam halted in the shadows of an old oak tree. "Well, I want to know if cheerleaders are born that way or brainwashed."

"What way?" Merilynn grinned.

"You know, all stupid and bouncy and wanting to, well, cheer. I mean, *where* does that come from?" Sam leaned forward, peering intently at Merilynn, as if she really expected an answer. "Well?" she said after a few seconds of silence. "Where does that cheery stuff come from?"

Merilynn shrugged. "I dunno."

"You're not one of them."

"No." Merilynn put her hand over her mouth to quell incipient giggles. "But then why am I here?"

Sam's eyebrow twitched. "That's obvious. You're here for the ghost stories. You'll put up with anything for a stupid ghost story."

"Ghost stories aren't stupid. Some of them are, sure, but the ones around here are great!"

Sam smiled. "Yeah, I understand. You're pursuing an interest. I mean one that involves your brain."

"Kinda."

"You're more like me. I mean, that's why we're here, right? We're both researching things. Come on," Sam added, starting to walk again. "Let's get this over with."

Merilynn hurried to catch up. "Maybe they're born that way."

"Huh?"

"The cheerleaders."

Sam nodded, leading them toward the boathouse. "I guess they must be. Have you noticed, though, there's more than one kind? At least three kinds."

"No. Tell me."

"Okay, first you've got all these airheads who are wearing makeup and padded bras and spray hair spray all over the place. They talk about boys non-stop, and all they want is to be popular. They snipe at each other a lot. They don't read, they don't think."

"That describes most of them," Merilynn admitted. "But the counselors are all cheerleaders."

"*College* cheerleaders. Smart, cream of the crop. Most of the girls here won't ever get past high school."

"What other kinds are there?"

"The rare kind is Eve. She's *such* a mystery."

"How is she a mystery? She doesn't snipe, she reads."

"That's what I mean. She has values; she's better than them. But she wants to be a cheerleader so bad it hurts."

"Eve is pure," Merilynn said. "She's real, and she's nice. I think she'll be a counselor here someday."

Sam's smile flashed in the moonlight. "Yeah. I don't know why she wants to waste her brain yelling rhymes. She's not like most of them."

"Who says she's wasting her brain?"

"Come on. You know how stupid all that jumping around and talking about 'team spirit' is. It's hokey."

"To you, it is." Merilynn hesitated. "And to me. But my ghost story thing probably seems hokey to you, and I can think of a lot less goofy things to do than study cheerleaders."

"Yeah, okay. Different strokes."

"Father says sometimes you just have to accept that things exist or that things happen, and accept you'll never know why."

"I disagree."

"Of course you do. You're going to be a detective when you grow up. You'll solve mysteries and catch criminals."

"Investigative reporter," Sam corrected.

"Okay."

"You know the difference, don't you, between a cop and a reporter?" she asked as they reached the boathouse and dock.

"You're such a snob, Sam. Of course I know the difference. Probably most of the airheads do too."

Up went the eyebrow. Down again. Sam nodded. "Okay, but say it again and I'll punch you."

All in all, a good reaction. "What's the third kind of cheerleader?"

They stepped onto the dock and approached a rowboat. Sam climbed down, then held her hand out to help Merilynn into the bobbing vessel before sitting down. "The third type is the alpha cheerleader."

"Alpha?" Merilynn undid the tie to the dock, then sat and took an oar before turning to look at Sam, on the bench behind her. "What do you mean?"

"Alpha is what they call the leader of a pack of dogs. Every group has alphas. They're dominant."

Merilynn nodded. "The super-bitches. The ones all the airheads want to impress."

"Exactly. It's like they're cloned or something. They all do their makeup just alike, and you never see them do it. It's as if they have it tattooed on. And if any of them are stuffing their bras, I haven't been able to tell."

Merilynn giggled. "You're checking out their boobs?"

"Not like *that!*" She paused. "The alphas give me the creeps."

"The Stepford Cheerleaders," Merilynn said, shivering as a cold-water breeze fingered her hair. "They look all bubbly and friendly, but they're hard-core bitches."

"They're who the airheads want to be." Sam dipped her oar into the water. "I'll row from the left, you take the right."

"Okay, let's go."

"Where?"

"Out there." Merilynn stared across the dark water, trying to make out Applehead Island, thinking she saw the dark hulk of it, but not sure. Maybe she just imagined she could see it.

"We're *not* going to the island," Sam said. "That's not part of the plan."

Merilynn shook her head. "No." She pointed at the

water west of the island, about halfway between it and the shore. "There. That's where the ghost lights are usually seen. I checked the maps. The center of town was about there."

"Okay," Sam said. "Start rowing."

Three

Oars dipped and stirred, black water lapped at the sides of the boat. Merilynn listened for imaginary wolves, knowing she wouldn't hear any chorus of lonely howls, but hoping anyway because it would make everything even more fun. *Spookier! Mysterious!* Somewhere, not too far away, an owl hooted, and its call was answered by softer *hoo-hoos* from farther off. Merilynn thought she heard the flap of wings over the water sounds.

Beyond midnight, the moon too low to cast much light, the forest felt alive, full of eyes hidden in darkness, peering at them from between the limbs of pines and clusters of oaks leaves. The trees were too far away and too dark for her to see any detail, but she could call up images from hundreds of twilights spent in her yard sitting alone, or with Father, watching faces appear in the shrubs and bushes and trees, as sunlight drained away. She imagined them now, leafy green faces. Momentarily, her thoughts turned to the island and the green, green eyes she'd gazed into, and wondered if they belonged to the Green Ghost and if he was a nature god, a real Green Man.

"So, what'd you think of Allie's ghost story?" Sam

asked, breaking Merilynn's reverie. "Do you think she saw Holly Gayle's ghost?"

She was trying to sound as if nothing was getting to her, not the story, not being alone on the haunted lake, but Merilynn could hear a faint quaver in her voice. She smiled to herself. "I don't know," she said, careful not to give the other girl any ammo; it was more fun to keep her nervous. "It was a pretty typical ghost story."

"What's *that* supposed to mean?" Sam feigned sarcasm.

"It means it's either more likely to be a made-up story, you know, like they saw some leaves blowing or a hunk of plastic or something and just *thought* it was a ghost. Or it means it's more likely true."

"Why?"

"Because Father says stories are patterned in truth. Real ghosts inspire the patterns in the stories. Allie's story fit just right." She paused, then added, "The clues are all there."

"Clues?" Sam's voice was suddenly a lot friendlier.

"Clues," Merilynn affirmed, feeling as if she'd caught a big fish, the word the hook.

"Such as?"

"Well, if somebody tells you a ghost talked to them, that's a clue that it's probably a fake story. Ghosts don't do that. I mean, they can talk, sort of, sometimes, but it's probably never personal. They don't call you by name, at least that's what Father says."

"They don't think."

"They? Oh, the ghosts?"

"Yeah."

"Father says they don't think, at least not much. They're always more like pictures or recordings than real people, he says."

"What do *you* think?"

"What's this? The third degree?"

"I'm investigating. So, tell me what you think."

"I think I don't know." Merilynn knew that was the only answer Sam would accept. If she told her the truth—that she thought, hoped maybe, that ghosts were sometimes real spirits, the other girl would go all sarcastic in a heartbeat. "I'm investigating too."

They paddled in silence for a few more minutes, slowly coming to verge upon the part of the lake Merilynn wanted to explore. She slowed her stroke, and Sam followed suit. "Start watching for lights."

Sam didn't say anything for several moments. Finally, she spoke. "You don't really expect to see anything, do you? I mean, the town's long gone. It can't light up. Back then, it wouldn't even have had electricity."

"They had candles and oil lamps." *Oops.* She regretted the words the moment she said them.

Sam snorted so loudly that the sound seemed to echo across the lake, silencing the crickets for half a minute. Merilynn hadn't even noticed them until they stopped, but when the seesaw chirping started again it seemed deafening.

"Candles and oil lamps don't light underwater," Sam remarked softly. She must have startled herself when she startled the crickets.

Eyes on the water, Merilynn said, "Lights can be ghosts, just like people can be ghosts."

"And lights can be reflections of stars or flashlights or the moon, just like a human ghost might be a plastic grocery bag flying in the wind. Or a piece of newspaper, or—"

"Look!" Lifting her oar from the water, Merilynn

stared at a dim amber glow that seemed to emanate from far below. She heard Sam set her oar down in the boat. "Do you see it? Straight down on the right."

"I see it. It must be a reflection."

"Of what?"

"I don't know. A star?"

"That's stupid."

"What?"

"It's stupid. You want to solve the mystery so bad that you'd rather think it's a reflection of a star than admit you don't know what the heck it is."

"I suppose *you* do?"

"I know it's not a star . . . Look. There's another one!"

"Oh, wow. There're more coming on! Do you see them?"

"Yes." Merilynn felt delight and a shiver of fear as the dim lights began to come to life, mostly faint, but some growing brighter and larger. Some looked deeper down than others. There were a dozen now, all varying shades of amber.

And then, a larger, closer cluster of lights began to appear. They were multicolored. "The stained glass," she said.

"What?"

"The colored lights. I read about that. An old church down there had a stained-glass window. It's, like, the *ultimate* sighting. Samantha, we are *so* lucky to see it." As she spoke, the glow brightened. It was small and far away, but so brilliant in its jewel tones of ruby, sapphire, gold, and emerald that it looked like a beacon.

"Holy crap," Sam murmured.

"I wonder if I could dive deep enough to see it without gear."

When Sam didn't reply, Merilynn tore her eyes away from the ghost lights for just an instant. Sam was staring at her. "What?"

"You're serious." There was awe in her voice. "You really want to go down there?"

Eyes back on the lights, Merilynn said, "Yes."

"It even makes *me* a little nervous, thinking of going down there."

"A *little* nervous? You sound like you're ready to pee your pants."

"Pretty much," Sam said softly. "I can't believe they didn't salvage a stained-glass window," she added, trying to sound businesslike.

"They did. It's at Greenbriar University. They put it in a window there."

Silence, long. Lights bloomed, some tracing street-like patterns like a tiny town seen from an airplane window at night. "If there's no window," Sam asked, "why can we see it?"

"It's a ghost of the window. Even if the real one was still down there, we couldn't see it. I mean, no divers are down there holding a spotlight behind a window."

"I know, I know. Merilynn?"

"What?"

"Yesterday, when we were coming back from the island, did you see anything?"

"No. I kept forgetting to look. Eve thought she saw some lights though. She told me. Did you see some?"

"Maybe. I didn't think about it much."

"You were thinking about the eyes we saw on the island?"

"No. That was just an animal."

"If you say so. What were you thinking about?" Below, a few tiny pinpoints of light moved along the dead roads. *Ghosts carrying lanterns? Or just lanterns? God, I want to find out!* As soon as she got home, she'd start bugging Father to let her take diving lessons.

"I was thinking about rowing and getting back before the bus brought the cheerleaders back from the field trip."

"Not the eyes?"

"Not much. That was just silly, that eye thing. Sillier than ghosts."

"But the eyes are a kind of ghost too. A nature ghost."

"Mountain lion. Cats' eyes glow in the dark."

"If you say so. I can't believe what we're seeing. This is so great!"

Sam stayed silent. Minutes passed and Merilynn just took in the lights, trying to memorize the positions, trying to see the pattern in the church window. Wind gusted, making her draw her coat closer and cross her arms for warmth. "Sam?"

Sam didn't answer.

"Sam?"

Hairs prickling up, Merilynn turned to look at Samantha. The girl was staring at something in the water on the other side of the boat. "What?" Merilynn asked, turning to face her. "What are you looking at?"

Sam didn't reply, just stared down.

Merilynn looked.

A girl, dead-white of face, dark hair waving in tendrils around her head, hovered just beneath the surface. Her mouth was open in a silent scream and her dark eyes bored into Samantha's.

Merilynn tilted forward for a better look, delicious tingles running up and down her spine. "When the ghost lights appear," she quoted, "it means Holly Gayle is going to walk again."

Sam bent farther over, farther and farther, until Merilynn could barely see Holly Gayle's face. Suddenly, she felt real fear. "Sam, be careful."

Sam didn't respond, but brought her hand up and over the side of the boat, letting her fingers touch the surface of the black water.

"Don't. It's a dead body!" Merilynn blurted, all the ghost talk chased away. Dead bodies scared her, not ghosts, so that's what this had to be.

A bloodless hand, blue white and delicate, suddenly snaked up, the fingers emerging from the lake, to slither between Sam's splayed fingers.

"No!" Merilynn cried as the dead fingers started to curl around Sam's. She reached out and yanked Sam away from the edge of the boat.

Both stared at the fingers as they uncurled, fingers that didn't shine but seemed lit from within, making them much too easy to see in the darkness. Just like the rest of Holly Gayle.

The hand, fingers upright, slowly, almost regally, slid beneath the water. The girls carefully peered over the side of the boat and watched the pale phantom turn and glide, eel-like, back into the depths, her white dress pluming out around her.

"That wasn't a dead body," Sam said.

"I know."

"It was her. Holly Gayle. Did you hear her?"

"No! She said something?"

"Maybe. In my head."

"What did she say?"

"She wanted me to go with her." Sam nodded toward the water. "Down there."

"Why?"

"She wanted to show me something."

"What?"

"I don't know. But if you hadn't pulled me back, well, I think maybe I would have gone overboard."

"That wouldn't be good."

"No. Thanks, Merilynn. Look, the lights are fading."

Merilynn looked. Even the stained-glass jewel was dimming. Smaller lights began to wink out, as if extinguished by unseen hands. "That was amazing!" Too elated to be afraid now, she giggled. "I can't wait to tell—"

"No. You can't tell. They'd think we were nuts—and we'd get in trouble, remember?"

"Not *them.* Father. I can't wait to tell him. And Eve. We can tell Eve."

"You can tell your father. I don't know about Eve. She might freak."

"She's part of this."

"Not anymore. She made that pretty clear when we got back to shore."

"True."

"Telling her will give her nightmares."

Merilynn nodded.

"You can't talk about this to anyone but me while you're here," Sam ordered.

Merilynn knew she was right, but it would be torture, keeping her mouth shut. "I know."

"And if you ever tell anyone what happened to me,

you're dead. Got it?" She picked up her oar, ready to go.

"I know," Merilynn murmured. Sam was being tough because she was scared, and that didn't bother her. "I won't embarrass you." She turned around, once again facing the prow, and grabbed her own oar.

Silently, they dipped the paddles into the water and began to turn the boat back toward camp. Merilynn looked into the water one last time. As she did, the stained-glass light wavered, then blinked out. "That was great."

"Yeah, great. Let's get out of here. One. Two. Three. Row!"

Greenbriar University

TODAY

Four

In the rolling hills of this part of coastal central California, autumn had started to dye the leaves of liquid-amber trees shades of red, orange, and gold by mid-October. In Caledonia, on the coast, not so far away, green still ruled, but here, only fifteen miles inland, wrapped in small mountains, nature was already painting a scene that delighted Kendra Phillips. Sitting at her desk, looking out at the lawn and gardens behind Gamma House, she felt a small stir of pleasure at the sight. She was pleased that she had noticed at all. The death of Eve Camlan, her roommate, had been a sorry blow, one that knocked awareness of her own life right out of her. She had spent the few weeks since the memorial service deep in her books. Her new sisters tried to talk to her about it, but she didn't want to talk, and they understood. Or seemed to.

Below, she saw Heather working in the herb garden that edged one side of the lawn. A couple of the J-clone cheerleaders were having an impromptu practice, working on some sort of acrobatic move that involved tumbling and landing in the splits. It looked painful, and she turned away because watching them reminded her of Eve.

There had been a short, typed suicide note, but no

body. There was talk that she'd left the note because she was running away. The girls all paid homage to this notion; it was what they said to Kendra most often. "You know, I'll bet she's just fine. I'll bet she decided to go to Europe for a year. Her parents wouldn't have approved. She couldn't tell them."

Bullshit. Kendra had seen her ghost. Genevieve Camlan had neither run away nor committed suicide. Something had happened to her. She'd been murdered. Kendra felt it in her bones.

She said nothing to anyone about her suspicions— *they aren't suspicions, I* know *I'm right!*—everything had been so cut-and-dry. The police in Greenbriar weren't even real cops; they were campus cops, even in town. The university funded them. *Owned them.* Sure, they'd asked some questions about Eve's state of mind and other friends, all the stuff that cops were supposed to ask, but it was as if no one even wanted to suggest foul play. Maybe it was because so much of it seemed to go on around Greenbriar.

That stuff the sisters said about Eve's parents not wanting her to go to Europe turned out to have some truth to it. When they came to collect her things, Kendra had come right out and asked them about it. It turned out that Eve had talked about going, briefly, but her parents discouraged it—and Eve hadn't argued, mainly because she didn't want her cheerleading skills to atrophy.

So, that was a possibility. Except that Kendra had seen her ghost. She'd *felt* her, felt the cold, seen that she wasn't solid, seen the anguish in her eyes, heard it in the voice that she heard with her mind, not her ears. She couldn't remember the words. But tell anyone about that? Funny farm time. *Kendra believes the story about the Phantom Hitchhiker too. And maybe the Hook.* She'd almost talked to Sam Penrose, but the would-be journalist had been silent on the subject. Who knew where her loyalties lay? Granny always said never to take chances around people you didn't know. It was good advice.

Someone knocked on the door, three light raps.

"Come in." Kendra marked her place in the folklore text and turned in her chair as the door opened. "Merilynn?"

"Am I interrupting you?"

"No, of course not. I'm just surprised to see you."

The girl with long red hair and brilliant green eyes stepped into the room and closed the door behind her. "I understand. We've never really talked and, well, you seemed so tight with Eve. You probably knew she didn't like me, so I've stayed away."

"Sit down."

"Thanks." Merilynn took the other chair. Eve's chair.

"She didn't dislike you, you know."

"She sure didn't want to be around me."

"No. You frightened her."

"I figured that was it. Back at camp, she was so frightened after we took a trip to the island."

"She told me about it."

Merilynn's eyes opened wide in surprise. "Really? I sort of thought she'd blocked the memory. Sam and I never even told her what we did the next night. I was going to, back then. I couldn't wait. Sam said it would freak her out, so I didn't."

She looked down at her hands, then back up at Kendra, her eyes sparkling with tears. One escaped, ran down her cheek, but she wiped it away as if it were nothing. Not at all like Eve. Merilynn looked fragile, but Eve had actually been the delicate one. "I'm so sorry she's dead. When I found out she joined this house, I had all these ideas about how I'd finally get to tell her about the ghost lights and seeing Holly and stuff." She paused. "You must think I'm nuts."

"Folklore's my thing. My family lived in Apple-head, then Greenbriar before moving to civilization. Most of my relatives—ancestors, mostly—worked here. I know the stories."

"Do you believe in ghosts?"

Kendra hesitated. She didn't dare reveal much to a stranger. "Let's say I'm open-minded. I've seen some things that might be called ghosts."

"Have you ever seen the ghost lights? The town under the lake?"

"No. I've never been there at night."

"Why not?"

"Well, I didn't go to the camp, and I didn't grow up in town."

Merilynn nodded. "They're amazing. I want to go back."

"Did you see Holly Gayle?"

The redhead nodded. "Sam and I both did." She giggled, putting her hand over her mouth. "But don't tell her I told you. The night we saw her, she swore me to secrecy." Another giggle. "She threatened to kill me if I ever dragged her name into any stories I decided I just had to tell."

Kendra smiled. "Well, I hope you'll tell me. Stories are my thing."

"I'd like to. I was wondering about something."

"What?"

"Well, just say no if you don't like the idea."

"What's the idea?"

"I'm in a room with two other girls. It's okay, but one's a cheerleader and the other just, well, sort of oozes sorority spirit. Know what I mean?"

Kendra nodded. "All too well."

"If you don't have a new roommate picked out, would I do? I'm pretty quiet. I don't take up much space." A slow, shy smile spread her face, revealing impish dimples. "I'm house-trained."

Kendra looked Merilynn up and down, mentally calling up Granny's rules. Though Merilynn struck her as offbeat, it was a good offbeat. She felt okay— Kendra wasn't picking up anything weird. Granny, she thought, would approve.

Standing up, she walked over to the other girl and held out her hand. "I think you'd make a great room-mate. Welcome."

Merilynn rose, but ignored her hand; instead, putting her hands on her shoulders and leaning forward to plant a quick kiss on Kendra's forehead, she said, "What time is it?"

"Almost noon."

"Crap. I've gotta run or I'll be late for class. Will you still be here at one?"

"Sure."

"Because we should talk a little more before you say yes. You need to know more about me. I'm a lit-tle weird."

Kendra smiled. "I'll be expecting you."

"Thanks!" Merilynn called as she fled the room.

Five

"There are four primary tastes," Malory Thomas said without consulting her index card of notes, "and four basic kinds of taste buds to taste them." She paused, glanced at Professor Tongue, then at the roomful of students. "The tastes are salty, sour, sweet, and"—another glance at Tongue—"spicy."

Girlish giggles erupted here and there.

"Since this is a public-speaking class," Professor Piccolo interrupted, "we won't criticize your alleged facts."

Malory batted her long black eyelashes. "I was joking. The fourth taste is bitter. I prefer spicy. Don't you, Professor?"

"A good point, as long as your talk is intended to be more amusing than instructional." Tongue looked flushed but managed a tight smile. "Continue, Ms. Thomas."

"Taste buds are little protuberances and you can see them with the"—pregnant pause, lower voice—"naked eye."

More giggles.

"How many of you have studied a tongue?" she asked throatily. "Your own, or your lover's?"

About half the women raised their hands, some

tentatively, many giggling, a couple shooting shame-
lessly straight up. The dozen males were all leaning
forward now, staring intently at Malory with big stupid grins on their faces and, undoubtedly, big
throbbing bones in their shorts.

"Ms. Thomas—"

"Let's talk about tastes," she continued, cutting
Piccolo off at the pass. "What does a banana taste
like? Primarily sweet. How about a tongue? Who
knows what a tongue tastes like? Some of you may
be able to taste your own tongue, if you've inherited
the ability to roll your tongue into different shapes
like this." She opened her mouth in an O, then stuck
her tongue out, curling it into a tube shape.

Just like the tube forming in the jocks' Levi's.

She unrolled her tongue and let it fold in against
itself, pivoting a little to make sure everyone, including the very good professor, could see. Then she
stopped and said, as brightly as a young Mary Tyler
Moore, "Okay, everybody, try it!"

"Ms. Thomas," Professor Tongue said in a voice
just a little deeper and rougher than normal, "I think
your demonstration is enough."

She smiled at him. "Please, you told us to get our
audience involved, Professor P."

"Yes, but . . ."

"But what?" She opened her eyes wide, all false
innocence, and batted the lashes some more. "Is
there something wrong with my report? Does it
bother you?"

Tongue, never rising from his desk in the right
corner—she knew he was in no shape to stand up—
looked uncomfortably at the class. All the females
stared at him; most of the males were watching Mal-

ory in her carefully chosen black skirt and matching pullover sweater. Her enameled rose sorority pin showed prominently on one breast, pinned so that the pink bud would make people think of sex even though her clothing, as always, was tasteful. And they rarely were smart enough to figure the trick.

"I'm not sure how appropriate . . ." Again, the professor's words trailed off.

"Professor?" she asked sweetly. "I don't understand. What's wrong?"

"Nothing, nothing. Go on." He looked at his hands as he spoke.

"I'm just talking about something every one of us has in our mouths. It's there every day of our lives, but we never think about what an amazing organ it is." She smiled like Miss America.

"Go ahead, Ms. Thomas. You're quite right."

"Now, everyone, stick out your tongues." She caught the eye of big blond quarterback Art Caliburn and wouldn't give it back. "Let's see what you can do."

She never tired of the power that came to her when people obeyed her, and she basked in it now as two-thirds of the class had their tongues out, and half of that number were gleefully miming various forms of oral sex. Malory cast her gaze over the group, finally coming to Samantha Penrose, unwilling to show any tongue, but perfectly willing to look her in the eye. That was a rush; hardly anyone ever dared try it, but Samantha never failed. That was the primary reason Malory had let her into the sorority, despite the others' trepidation about the journalism major's loyalty.

Sam Penrose was special in many ways. A natural leader, she could go far in the world as an alumna of

Fata Morgana. She would do great things for the sisterhood if she truly understood loyalty. And if not, she would probably make a fine sacrifice to the Forest Knight. Right after Eve Camlan escaped her fate, Malory had decided to use Sam as a replacement during All Hallows Eve, the next likely night for such a sacrifice. But in the weeks since Eve had left, Samantha had refrained from digging into the "suicide," and she'd made it clear to Malory that this was because of her loyalty to the Gamma sisters.

That was promising. Very promising. She nodded at Sam, Sam nodded back, almost imperceptibly. Sam was going to be fun. Later. One way or another.

Two seats over was Merilynn Morris, who was about to become a Fata Morgana, though she didn't know it yet. Merilynn, looking puckish yet angelic—*as she should*—was completely involved with her own tongue, looking cross-eyed at it. She had stuck it out as far as she could, curled the sides up, and was now trying to touch her nose. Malory smiled. Though the girl couldn't quite reach her goal, she definitely had latent talents.

Merilynn brought her tongue back down, still cross-eyed with interest, and stuck it straight out. It was a healthy shade of dark pink with a pointed tip.

Just like her mother's.

"Ms. Thomas," the King of Tongues said, "I think that's enough time for your demonstration."

"But, Professor Piccolo," she said, turning to him and wetting her lips, "I saw everyone but you try it. Can you curl *your* tongue?"

The classroom went silent. Twenty shades of red flashed over Piccolo's face before he spoke. "As your instructor, I respectfully decline."

"Please?" came a couple of girlish voices from somewhere in the sea of desks. Giggles erupted like brushfires.

"Finish your talk, please, Ms. Thomas. Class is almost over."

Malory nodded, seeing the time. She had barely begun to warm them up, hadn't even started to weave her spells over the room. "Professor, I need more time to finish my speech. You have to admit, I'm not getting my full thirty minutes today."

"I'd think you'd find that to be a relief, Ms. Thomas."

Students chuckled. Malory didn't like that a bit. "Professor, I want the best grade I'm capable of getting. I'd like another chance to excite you with my talk."

Now they giggled. That was more like it.

"We don't really have time." He hesitated. "You may finish your speech after class. I have a free period."

"Can we stay?" one of the guys asked. Others seconded the notion.

"Of course," Piccolo said quickly.

Malory smiled, knowing he preferred to have witnesses when dealing with any female student. It was a well-known fact that young ladies frequently made appointments for private discussions during his office hours. Though he kept his tongue hidden, and played down his reputation as rumor, the girls—and an occasional guy—wanted the truth. He'd told Malory he always engaged straight male student assistants, and always kept one in his office when a coed came calling. "You know, just like a male gynecologist keeps a nurse in the exam room when a patient climbs into the saddle and puts her feet in the stirrups." The Tongue liked westerns. Malory found it cute most of the time.

The buzzer sounded, ending the class. No males dared stand. Behind his desk, Piccolo said, "Class dismissed. Anyone who would care to hear the rest of Ms. Thomas's talk, please come back by one-fifteen."

A few of the girls stood up and milled around. Malory smiled at Art Caliburn, then smiled more broadly as Merilynn Morris approached, hugging her books in front of her breasts like a little girl.

"Hello, Sister," Malory said with as much warmth as she was capable of.

"Hi, Malory."

"Class dismissed!" Piccolo repeated. "All of you, out of here. You can return in fifteen minutes. Shoo!"

Merilynn bestowed her Madonna-like smile. "You gave him an erection," she said softly. "That's why he's still sitting there and telling us to leave."

Malory nodded. "Sweetie, I gave them *all* erections. Look behind you. The boys are all holding their book bags in front of them."

Merilynn looked, turned back to Malory, beaming. "How'd you do that?"

"What?"

"Give them erections. So fast."

"They're college boys. They get erections just from breathing."

"You didn't, ah, *do* anything?"

"Whatever do you mean?"

"Nothing. It just sort of seemed like you wove a spell or something."

Not yet. But I will. "Thank you. That means I gave a good talk. Let's get out of here before the professor throws us out."

They walked outside and down the hall to the water fountain. Merilynn drank, then said, "I wish I could stay for the rest of your talk."

"You can't stay? Really?"

"No, not today. I have to run. I'm sorry."

Malory smiled. "I'm sorry too. I'll see you later, at the house."

"Okay. Good luck."

Merilynn walked quickly down the hall toward the exit. Malory watched her with mixed emotions. All in all, it was probably best that she left; she was too aware of the magic and until she became a Fata Morgana, keeping her in the dark was a good idea.

Six

"I'm back," Merilynn said after Kendra opened the door, "and before you say yes, I should tell you I'm kind of weird."

Kendra smiled. "Sometimes weird is good."

"Or not."

Closing the door, Kendra went to the little fridge by her desk and took out two bottles of water. She handed one to Merilynn, who had already flopped onto Eve's desk chair.

"Thank you." Merilynn got the top off in record time and started to drink.

"Did you run all the way back? You sound out of breath."

"And I'm thirsty, too!" She took another drink and set the bottle on the desk. "That's so good. Anyway, I did run. Well, I sort of trotted. The class ran over a little. Malory's in it."

"You're in a class with a senior?"

"It's public speaking. It's totally mixed. Freshmen, seniors, jocks, brains. I'm there because I'm bad at it. I mumble."

"No, you don't."

"Only in front of groups."

"Oh." Kendra took a pull on her own bottle.

"Malory is the last person I'd expect to find in a public-speaking class. I mean, what does she need it for?"

Merilynn savored the moment. "She doesn't need it," she said very softly. "She *likes* it. She's an exhibitionist."

"Really?"

"I'm almost positive. She gave a speech on tongues. Every guy in the room had a woody. It was hysterical. She even made simple facts about taste buds sound dirty."

"Tell me more."

"I will. Later, okay? I want to have our talk and confess all my weird shit to you and find out if you'll still have me."

"Confess away."

"Do you remember when they made us all announce our majors and I didn't want to give one?"

"Sure, I remember. I liked that you didn't care what anyone else thought." She hesitated. "And you should know that it helped Eve. She didn't have a major picked out either and was very embarrassed. You made her feel better."

"That's good." Merilynn smiled. "Poor little Evie. She was afraid of everything when she was a kid. I guess she never got over it? Being easily spooked, I mean?"

"She seemed fine," Kendra said after looking toward the ceiling and considering. "Maybe a little on the timid side. I didn't know her very long, but I think she might have been the only person I've ever met who honestly seemed, I don't know . . ."

"Earnestly good? Kind?" Merilynn asked. That's how she remembered her from Applehead.

Kendra nodded. "Exactly. And that worried me at first. Most people that come on that way are seriously *not* good or kind. I like people to have some faults. Makes them human, like me. Know what I mean?"

"Yes, I do." Merilynn had liked Kendra the first time they'd met, but she'd stayed away to spare Eve. She saw now that she'd been right about her—Kendra was a good guy. "I saw how you watched out for Evie. You're just like Sam."

Kendra raised a hand. "Stop! Hold it right there. I don't know if I want to be just like Sam. I admire her, but she's a little scary."

"Sam? Scary?" Merilynn loved Kendra's reaction. It was typical. She'd seen it as a kid in camp and she'd seen it at Greenbriar.

"She's, uh . . ."

"Intense?"

Kendra nodded. "That's it. I hope I don't come off like that."

"No, you're much more approachable." She laughed. "I don't think I'd want you pissed off at me though!"

Kendra laughed. "Can I take that as a compliment?"

"Yes. See, if I'd said that to Sam, she would have just said, 'Thank you,' instead of asking if it was a compliment. You have better social skills. But don't let her scare you. She's all warm and fuzzy inside. She'd never admit it, though. She watched out for Eve like you did."

"Thank you."

"So, do you want to hear my faults?"

"Okay. But why'd you bring up your major? When they pressed you, you said chemistry, right?"

"I think so. Yes. Maybe I said several things. I

like to be creative with my answers. But I do like chemistry."

"So, what's your horrible secret? A traveling lab? You're a mad scientist in training?"

Merilynn finished her water, feeling good about coming to Kendra. "I'm taking some normal chemistry classes, but it's a more old-fashioned kind of chemistry I'm *really* interested in. They don't have classes in it. I study on my own and take classes related to it. Like chemistry and botany."

"So, what is it?"

"Well, it's weird. And I don't have a suitcase full of chemicals, but I *do* have a box full of the stuff I study on my own. It's weird." She watched Kendra for a reaction, but got none. "Don't worry, I don't make crack or grow pot in my closet."

Kendra smiled. "So tell me the worst."

"Herbs. I study herbal medicine." She studied more than medicine, but didn't think she should say so. Not yet anyway.

"Well, that's fascinating!" Kendra shook her head. "There always used to be an herbalist in our family. My granny's kind of a half-assed herbalist. She learned a lot when she was young, but never practiced, except for tacking rosemary on doors to keep ghosts out, and things like that. Anyway, I have no problem with your herbs." She paused. "They don't smell gross or anything?"

"Some smell gross, but you'd have to open the containers and stick your nose in to know it."

"Well, then I don't even know why you thought I'd think that was a fault. You know I'm mainly studying folklore-type subjects, right?"

"Yes. That's one of the reasons I thought we might

get along. I'm interested in those things too." Merilynn hesitated. "But my herbs and stuff? I have to tell you. Sometimes I do weird things with them."

"Hey, as long as you don't turn 'em into incense and smoke up the room, I'm cool, otherwise. I just hate smoke."

"Even smoke that smells good?"

"Yeah. It messes with my sinuses."

Merilynn loved incense and had to hide her disappointment. "No smoke."

"So what do you do? Mix them? Turn them into powders and mysterious concoctions to cure warts?"

"Yes, pretty much. I can cure a wart. Do you have one?"

Kendra looked confused for a second, then smiled. "No. No warts. What else can you cure?"

"What've you got?"

"A craving for chocolate."

"I can cure that."

"Now?"

"I don't have my lab with me, but if I go get my stuff, I'll cure you quick."

"Okay."

Merilynn walked to the door. "I'll be right back. If it's okay."

"Of course it is. You live here now." Kendra consulted her wristwatch. "I have a class in forty-five minutes, so you'll be on your own moving in."

Merilynn laughed. "You're so nice. I was just going to get the cure for your craving. But if you don't mind, I'm done with classes for the day. I'd love to move in."

"Not a problem."

Merilynn started to open the door.

"Wait. I have one question."

She pushed the door closed. "What?"

"Do you have any other quirks?"

"I sleep in the nude."

"Oh . . . okay . . ."

Seeing Kendra's discomfort, Merilynn quickly said, "Just kidding."

"Good. I'm not sure I'd ever get used to that!"

"Do *you* have any quirks?"

"Me?" Kendra said. "I'm a regular paragon of virtue."

"So you don't keep Limburger cheese in your underwear drawer or anything weird like that?"

Her new roommate chuckled. "No, but now I'm worried. What made you think of such a thing?"

"I have no idea. But I'll be right back with the cure for chocolate craving."

"It doesn't taste nasty or anything, does it?"

"Heck no. There's only one cure for a chocolate craving, and I have a whole shoe box of it in *my* underwear drawer. Cadbury bars. Two dozen of them. Well, four have gone missing in the last two days. That's another reason I want out of the monkey house down the hall. Those two little bitches are going through my stuff and stealing from me! One of them got into my herbs and tried to smoke some. That girl turned green."

"What did she smoke?"

"Mugwort."

Kendra snorted. "If she mistook that for pot . . ." She shook her head, smiling.

"I don't really *know*. She didn't admit it. I could smell it, she was sick, and half my supply was gone."

"People used to burn mugwort to get rid of ghosts," Kendra said, locking eyes with Merilynn.

"They still do." The two studied each other. It felt good.

"Then go, before they steal any more chocolate. Better bring the whole box back just to be safe. I'm not a thief."

Merilynn made her Gollum face and voice. "What's the cheerleader got in its pocketses?"

Merilynn left, closing the door behind her. Kendra's laughter trailed her. As she approached her old room, she wondered how Kendra would react if she knew *everything* she did with her herbs and crystals, and vials of oil, and decided, overall, she felt pretty optimistic.

Seven

"Tongues are amazing," purred Malory Thomas, pleased that nearly all of Professor Piccolo's public-speaking class had come back and were silently hanging on her every word. "They have no bones, and yet we can make them go stiff." She batted her lashes at Art Caliburn. He might be a pleasant ride. "The tongue and the penis are the only organs capable of this feat—"

"Ms. Thomas, this isn't sex ed."

The protest was weak, at best, and she ignored him. "The feminine equivalent of the penis does share these qualities, but it's such a tiny little thing, you can see why I don't really include it with the larger organs. Of course, ladies, we all know that that's one place where size doesn't matter."

The class was too excited now to giggle. As she spoke aloud, she silently wove little power spells over the room, harnessing the sexual energy that emanated from the students in threads so thick it seemed to ooze from their pores, pulling it all together, male and female energy, into one big psychic jolt waiting to happen. Pulling and pulling, slowly, tenderly, like good foreplay. "These organs have something else in common. Does anyone know what that might be?"

The room was silent but for the sound of breathing. Students, male and female, stared hard at her. Piccolo said nothing, but she could feel his eyes caressing her ass. "The organs are the most sensitive on our bodies." She glanced at the professor but he was looking at his hands, folded together on his desk, no doubt to keep them from trembling. Smiling, she turned back to the students. "Who wants to take a guess? Of the penis and the tongue, which one's tip is the most sensitive? Art? Do you know?"

The quarterback reddened as she drilled him with her eyes. Nostrils flared, as did his aura. Normally, she purposely paid no attention to auras—she didn't need to see them to know how people felt, and they could be quite annoying—but his grew so strong and spiky that it couldn't be ignored. She wished Merilynn had remained. It would be interesting to know if the girl could see the pulsing purple-red colors that surrounded him. She approached his front-row seat and stood close enough to bask in his energy, to feed on it. "Art? Do you know?"

"Know what?" he managed.

"Which is more sensitive? The tip of your tongue or the tip of your penis?"

His jaw worked, but like Piccolo, he seemed to have run out of words. She backed off. "Anyone else?" She scanned faces, noted that there were some new ones mixed in, like Spence Lake, Art's buddy.

"The tongue," a female voice said, "is the most sensitive organ."

"Samantha Penrose," Malory said with delight, spotting the young woman at the rear of the room, mostly hidden behind Frank Steiner, the incredible hulking golden boy of the Greenbriar wrestling squad.

"Are you sure?" she asked, walking back to see her up close.

"I'm sure," Sam said.

"Then I'm happy to tell you that you're correct." Up close, she could sense a strong pulse of sensuality emanating from her young sorority sister, but Sam Penrose was holding it close, not letting it escape. It was hard to read, so Malory let herself see Sam's aura. Held tight to her body, it was shades of orange, red, and purple, a narrow silhouette. Her normal aura, golden in tone, shot farther out, surrounding her body like the sun's corona. *A control freak.* Slightly disturbed by the strength and color of the Penrose aura—*I should have looked her over this way before*—Malory reached down and touched Sam's shoulder, weaving a special spell as she did.

Samantha caught her breath as the narrow orange-red-purple stripe of sexuality doubled in size. She looked at Malory with sharp eyes muddled with a lust she no doubt didn't know she possessed. Malory quickly withdrew her hand and turned, walking to the front of the class. When she arrived in front of the blackboard and turned around, Sam had already begun to pull the sensual colors back to their former size. *Amazing strength.*

Excited by the brute willpower of the girl, she knew she wouldn't rest until she broke it down. That would come in time. "We use our tongues for many purposes besides taste," she began. "And animals use them for even more things than we do. Cats and dogs use it as a ladle to scoop up water. Watch a cat sometime and you'll see something amazing. Cats don't do this—" She extended her tongue and dipped it down and up, as if she were lapping water. She paused, soaking up the doubled energy in the room, taking it, winding it into a ball of psychic sexual power.

Finally, she continued. "Cats do it a different way. Like this—" Now she slowly pushed her tongue out from between her lips and curled it under, down, and then up into her mouth, like a butterfly sipping nectar from a flower.

At the back of the room, something stirred in the air. Still sensing auras, she followed the feeling and saw brilliant white light flashing around Frank Steiner. His eyes squeezed closed, his mouth in a grimace, his big body was stretched and stiff at his desk. Malory watched his secret orgasm until everyone else turned to see what she was looking at.

Spence Lake started to laugh first. Fearing he'd break the tension in the room, she wrapped his tongue in silent words, silencing him, turning his thoughts—and the other students'—back to their own desires. No one even noticed when Steiner grunted and looked around, his face the color of embarrassment.

"Animals use their tongues to clean their own fur or to groom one another. Cats, again, are the creatures to watch. They excel at it. We humans sometimes lick one another as well, but not to clean, unless it involves sex and food. Who hasn't fantasized about licking whipped cream off a lover?"

Sexual tension flared even higher. She gathered it to her and looked back at Piccolo—his reaction was so strong she could feel it from behind. He was still looking at his hands.

"So, when we lick another person, we are really showing affection or desire. We do this with something as simple as a kiss when we let our tongues twine and dance with our lover's."

The tension was so thick now that the air seemed fogged and she could see the ball she'd accumulated, as big as a basketball, glowing before her. She wondered if Merilynn would have seen it as well. Looking over the faces as she spoke, she saw that a young man with dreadlocks—she couldn't remember his name—appeared to see it, though it probably just looked that way. Most likely he was staring at her—but not at her face, as the others were. "Animals," she continued, dismissing him as she prepared to release the ball, "do the same thing, using their tongues to greet one another or their owners. Dogs are so good at this that sometimes women have been known to encourage them to lick their genitalia." Weaving words of power, weaving a fog around the ball so that no one would remember exactly what happened, she continued to talk. "Of course, dogs' tongues are soft. If you prefer a rougher sensation, you can pour a little tuna oil over your clitoris to get your pussycat to—"

Now! The ball of energy burst like fireworks, shooting up and out and over the students, raining across them. Every student body in the room started to arch. Quickly, Malory stepped among the desks to bask in it.

Men grunted, experiencing orgasms longer than they imagined possible. *Too bad they won't remember why their shorts are soaked.* Some shrieked, regardless of gender. From Piccolo's desk came a hearty "Yeehaw!" a cry familiar to her. One girl, then two, ululated Xena style, and at least half the students invoked deities in true porno film fashion. One student, Diana Peckerwood, had thrown her large head back on her large body and breathlessly cried,

"Yes! Yes! Yes!" at least two dozen times in a row, sounding like an ad for shampoo.

She looked at Art Caliburn and Spence Lake, saw grimacing pleasure. She looked at the guy with dreads, amused to see his eyes closed, his wide mouth spread in a huge blissful grin. *He could be fun too.* If she could get past his mellowness, into his animal side, he might be a true tiger.

She walked up to Samantha Penrose, pleased to see the closed eyes. The purples spiked through the golden aura, but they were controlled, as was Sam, who made no sound, but looked to be concentrating intensely. Beneath her lids, her eyes jittered back and forth. Orgasmic blush spread up from her neck, over her cheeks, and as Malory watched, even to her forehead.

And then she opened her eyes and looked into Malory's. Her gaze was straight and sharp with curiosity. In a hoarse voice, she asked, "What did you do?"

"Nothing. What did you do?"

"Yeehaw!" cried Professor Tongue, a second time. Frank Steiner stiffened again.

Sam Penrose started to look around the room. Malory put her hand on top of her shining dark hair, sending her into another orgasm, this one beyond control. Sam screamed like a horror movie queen. Malory put her hand over the girl's mouth, and was nearly bitten before she'd woven her screams into silent ones.

An orgy, she thought as she examined the other students one by one. An orgy with Tongue and Caliburn, with the guy with the dreadlocks, with Brittany, and most of all, with Samantha Penrose, the most controlled and most strongly orgasmic human female she had ever encountered. *Such a strong-willed creature, I should tame her a bit.*

Visions of handcuffs and hot candle wax dancing in her head, Malory strolled from the orgasmic classroom, knowing that as soon as she was gone, the spell would die away, leaving lots of confused but very relaxed and happy people to wonder what had happened.

Eight

"Puckwudgies," proclaimed Professor Daniel Mc-Cobb. Light chuckles erupted behind him as he wrote the word on the board, and died off as he turned around, his big old lion's head with its mane of white hair limning his face as if a thousand volts had just fed through him.

He smiled at this class, his favorite, Folklore of California. He had learned to smile years ago, after Vera pointed out that his rocky face intimidated students. That was good, of course, but unnecessary most of the time. With his puckish blue eyes and tangled Einsteinian brows, his little St. Nick–pursed mouth, Vera said he was part Santa and part Satan.

The classroom door opened and Jimmy Freeman, of the peaceful smile and wild dreadlocks, came in, looking a little sheepish. Jimmy was a good kid, so McCobb let him slip in without commenting on his tardiness.

"Puckwudgies," he repeated instead, tipping his head back to look at the students from over his reading glasses. "Are any of you familiar with the word?"

Kendra Phillips was the one to raise a hand.

"Yes?"

"It's a native word meaning 'little people of the

forest,' and refers to nature elementals. They're a variation on fairies or gnomes."

"Yes, exactly. The word is found throughout the states in various but similar forms. For example, in the Algonquin dialect of the northeastern states, they were Puckwudjinies, which translates into 'little vanishing people.' They considered these beings to be somewhere between this world and the spirit world, usually invisible, but occasionally seen.

"It's interesting to note the resemblance to European words. Shakespeare's Puck in *A Midsummer Night's Dream* is a good example. He's an elf of sorts, a king of the forest. It probably derives from the old Gothic word, Puke, which is a name for minor spirits in Teutonic dialects." The name brought expected giggles. He waited for the students to get it out of their systems, then continued. "There's also the Dutch word, Spook, which translates to ghost, and German's Spuk, which means goblin. The Irish variant is Pooka. All these creatures refer to spirits with the ability to vanish. Perhaps, somehow, in history yet to be figured out, the word traveled between here and there long before Columbus. Perhaps it's a coincidence." He winked at the class. "But there are no coincidences."

As he spoke, he pondered mentioning his sighting of the Greenbriar Ghost. Despite what he'd told his wife and son—that the leafy visage with glowing green eyes was the work of mischievous students— he thought that, perhaps, he'd really seen something supernatural, the face behind the myth. *Or I could just be going senile.*

"Our local Puckwudgies are of the same mint as all of those supernatural beings. Here in America, the natives weren't the only ones who told tales of these creatures. Immigrants brought tales of fairies and elves and gnomes with them, and usually kept those words. There are variations. New England has the Gentry, for example. Do any of you know other names?"

A few variations were given, but not the one he was looking for. "There is a little-known variant on these creatures, one that very closely resembles the natives' Puckwudgies. The Greenjacks. Have you heard the term?"

Silence was his answer.

"Greenjacks is a term brought from Scotland to California by immigrants in the nineteenth century. A Greenjack is a nature elemental, a frightening spook with a penchant for stealing the bodies of humans, but only ones who can see them. They can inhabit nonseers, but then they are forever cut off from their own kind, and they are too social for that."

He paused. "Fortunately for us poor humans, seers are very rare. Greenjacks are of the spirit world far more than the physical. Hence, the story goes, they long for physical sensations, to taste food, to touch, to lust. Like most nature spirits, they are rarely evil in and of themselves, but they *are* hedonists and tricksters, and body snatchers.

"Their power ebbs in winter, and grows throughout spring and summer, to peak in the fall, on All Hallows Eve. That is the one night of the year that they can do their dirty work. They can steal bodies then and affect the world in other ways. The Greenjacks built a physical being on that night, built it of wood, bark, and leaves. It was called Big Jack, and it could capture the seer for them so that they could steal the body. Big Jack, being physical yet supernatural, is a Green Man form. Green Men range from all plant, like Jack, to blooded gods like Pan, to humans who have qualities that make them one with nature. Robin Hood is a human Green Man."

He looked around the room, seeing rapt attention on most of the faces. Even students who took this course because it was a fairly easy one with no requirements were inevitably drawn into it since it was about California, and that was where they lived. This class and his always overflowing Urban Legends class were fun. He'd told Vera he enjoyed them because they generally made good students out of bad ones. *If you give someone something to study that actually interests them,* he told her whenever he came home pleasantly surprised by an underachiever, *they discover they are capable of more than they ever expected.*

"Professor?" Kendra had her hand up.

"Yes?"

"Are the Greenjack stories still extant?"

"You mean, does anyone believe in Greenjacks anymore?"

"Yes, or at least tell the stories?"

"My son actually lives in a southern California town founded by a family who claimed to have seers in their bloodlines. The stories spread from them, as well as from other Scots immigrants throughout the country. It was a story peculiar to a small area of the Highlands, and it is still told here and there. The family who founded the town of Santo Verde still lives there. I expect they tell the tales." He winked at her. "Who knows? Maybe some even see the Greenjacks." He laughed.

"Now, why am I telling you about Greenjacks when I started with the midcoastal Puckwudgies, you ask? Because they are virtually identical. There is really only one difference. The Puckwudgies of the natives didn't build a Big Jack, nor was there a single Green Man form as a nature diety, although there were stories of a dangerous trickster spirit of great power that lived in the woods and had glowing emeralds for eyes. Local natives had multiple spirit gods, one for green growing things, one for the soil, one for rocks, and so forth. But the many became one when Europeans arrived. They became a Green Man form, a mix of Big Jack and a supernatural form that is able to affect our world. This form is not restricted to Halloween night, but it is powerful at that time, as are all Green Men. This form is known for its green glowing eyes and its ability to shriek, a trait perhaps added by those who enjoyed banshee tales.

"You all know this form. Even if you're from somewhere else, you've surely heard the stories of the Greenbriar Ghost by now. He lives in Applehead Forest and is usually called, simply, the Green Ghost. Sometimes, he is the Forest Knight. He is reputed to hold court in the old chapel in the woods—and I *know* you've all heard of that trysting spot by now—and to be seen, as often as not, holding his green head by its tendrils of green hair. And that's extremely interesting to a folklorist because it's an example of European folklore mixing with native stories. The tale from the British Isles may be based in truth, there is no way to be certain, though the Forest Knight is certainly a mythical aspect. Have any of you guessed what I'm talking about? Just speak, no hands necessary."

"It sounds familiar," Kendra said finally.

"If I use another term, then, I think you'll know. Our Greenbriar Ghost is occasionally referred to as the Green Knight as well as Forest Knight."

"Sir Gawain and the Green Knight!" Kendra nearly exploded with the words. "I should have known that."

"You did know it, my dear. What Kendra said is the title of a lyric poem about one of King Arthur's knights. It is a story of honor. The Green Knight rides his horse into Arthur's court and demands that a knight fight him, a blow for a blow. Finally the honorable Sir Gawain takes the challenge and ends up beheading the Green Knight, who does not avoid the blow. Calmly, the knight picks up his head, and the head speaks, telling Gawain that he must meet him in a year.

"A year passes and Gawain rides out to meet a certain death. Nearing the home of the Green Knight, a chapel in the woods, he meets a minor lord who takes him in until the day arrives for the battle. While staying with the lord and his lady, Gawain is tempted by her each day with a kiss, but he never acts upon the urges she arouses. Each night, the lord and Gawain tell one another everything that happened that day. Gawain tells him everything. One day, the lady gives Gawain her scarf to wear into battle with the Green Knight. This, Gawain takes and fails to tell the lord.

"When the day arrives, Gawain meets the Green Knight and stands to take his blow, expecting to die. But the Green Knight, who is allowed three tries, stops short of his neck twice and the third time barely nicks him. Then he lets him go free. Gawain finds out that the Green Knight and the generous lord are one and the same, and that the nick was punishment for keeping the scarf a secret.

"Any questions?"

The usual suspect raised her hand.

"Yes, Kendra?"

"I've only heard of the Greenbriar Ghost being

headless because my grandmother told me the old stories. I haven't heard it like that here on campus."

"That's a very good point and an excellent example of how our myths keep evolving. Someone, long ago, came here and told the Arthurian legends. The green-eyed trickster spirit of the natives of this area transformed into the Green Knight, always headless, then slowly began being seen with his head on occasion. Nowadays," he added with a nostalgic yearning, "I'm afraid our trickster usually has his head firmly on his shoulders." He smiled. "I encourage you all, when you have children of your own, to tell the tale with the knight—Forest or Green—holding his head by its leafy hair."

Kendra waved a hand. He nodded.

"Professor McCobb, I thought the trickster was represented as Coyote or Raven by the Chumash and other local tribes."

"Generally speaking, that's true, but there are always variations. The local natives had long been distant from the primary tribes and developed their own trickster form over time."

"Why?" Kendra asked. "Do you think there was a reason for them to change it?"

McCobb loved the question. "I suspect there's usually a reason behind everything. People here still tell of seeing the green eyes, sometimes even a green ghostly form. Perhaps there is something in the woods, maybe some odd refractions of light, or some local birds, that give basis for the stories. Maybe the tradition is now simply carried on by tricksters of flesh and blood, out to scare people just for fun. Yes, Jimmy?"

"All the deaths we have around here," the young man said, "play into the stories, don't they?"

"Yes, they do. We have the serial-killer story, dating back over a century, and that's a mythic form more in line with the Hook and Phantom Hitchhiker stories. Obviously, we occasionally do have bad people lurking in our woods, and that feeds the myths. We are developing the serial-killer myth both separate from the Greenbriar Ghost and *as* the Greenbriar Ghost or Forest Knight. It will be interesting to check in thirty or forty years to see how the stories have grown or died away."

He looked around the room. "Or maybe the Greenbriar Ghost *is* the predator, directly or indirectly. The latter, I think, is far more likely. We've had rumors of human sacrifice since the region was settled. Some may be true, and if so, someone is sacrificing to some form of the ghost." He cleared his throat. "Many someones, I should say, since these stories go back so far. There is another myth that intertwines with our Greenbriar Ghost and may also meld together with the other stories someday. Guesses?"

"The ghost of Holly Gayle?" someone asked timidly.

"That's right. Next time, we'll talk about our most enduring recent ghost story, one barely old enough to be mythic, but it bears all the earmarks. Many of you probably even know people who claim to have seen her. Do any of you ladies happen to be Gamma sisters?"

Kendra raised her hand.

"Holly is often said to roam the halls of her old sorority house. You must be fairly familiar with this ghost story."

"Yes," Kendra said in an uncharacteristically somber voice. "Yes, I'm acquainted with the stories."

Something in her demeanor intrigued him, but he hid it. "We're going to stay on the subject of the Greenbriar Ghost stories today, but next week we'll talk about Holly. Kendra, perhaps you can make an appointment to see me during office hours? I'd like to compare notes so that our class on our own campus ghost is as complete as possible."

Kendra wet her lips and nodded.

"Now then, let's get back to the habits of the Puckwudgies and the King Puck that the early settlers bestowed upon them."

The rest of the session, he kept wondering what a girl like Kendra Phillips was doing in that house. It worried him.

Nine

"That little stunt you pulled today wasn't very nice," Professor Tongue said, as he stood back and let Malory enter his cottage.

She ignored him, shedding clothes like snakeskin as she crossed his living room and passed through the little dining room. By the time she opened his refrigerator, she was nude. She found a can of whipped cream on the top shelf, then turned and looked at the Tongue. He had closed the drapes, which was rather boring of him, but in these times of sexual politics, she supposed it was necessary. Now he approached, gathering her clothes along the way. At the kitchen threshold, he picked up her black thong.

"Carry it in your mouth," she ordered.

"Why?"

"To turn me on."

"Yes, m'lady." He grabbed the crotch in his teeth and stood there staring at her like a big dumb hound dog.

No, not a hound. A bulldog. Bulldogs always seemed to have their tongues hanging out. "Use your tongue like a hook to carry them."

He even cocked his head like a dog. "What?"

"I want to see your tongue."

He took the panties out of his mouth and grinned. "You've been absolutely nuts about tongues lately."

"I'm always nuts about your tongue, you know that."

"Yes, but you've changed. You don't just want me to use it on you. I think you're developing a fetish."

She turned and grabbed a jar of maraschino cherries from the second shelf, then, hands full, used her ass to close the door. She grinned. He was right, to some extent, but he didn't know the half of it. He had inspired the glamour she had used to frighten Eve Camlan, the twisted face of the Forest Knight with a tongue Pan himself would kill for. "Well, Professor, if I'm becoming a tongue freak, then it's all your fault."

She passed him and he followed close behind, a puppy waiting for his treat. In the bedroom, she turned and looked at him. "Why aren't those panties on their new hook?"

"Huh? Oh." He stuck his tongue out and snagged them up. "'ow's dis?"

"Fine. Don't talk with your mouth full." She set the canned cream and the cherries on the nightstand and pulled back the boring bedspread—shades of blue in geometric patterns—and blankets, letting them all drop to the carpet at the foot of the bed.

Climbing on, she spread out comfortably and grabbed the jar of cherries. "Get undressed, Professor Piccolo. You're going to practice bobbing for apples." She opened the jar and took out a cherry.

He watched, eyes glazing, pants tenting, as she held it between her fingers and put it in her mouth. She sucked the juice off, then held it up by the stem and showed it to him. "It's almost Halloween, you know." His eyes watched every movement as she put the cherry in the designated receptacle, then took another and another from the jar. "A baker's dozen," she told him as she squeezed the last one in. "Think you can get them all out?"

The panties dropped, forgotten, as he started undressing, his eyes never wavering from the cherries' new home. He removed his shirt and pants, revealing a broad chest covered with curly light brown hair. Unfortunately, his waist was the same width as his chest and his hips had love handles, but it all gave him a pleasant teddy bear or puppy dog—it depended on her mood—appearance. Below a ridiculous bush of nether hair, his little man stood at attention. Too bad, she thought, it was such a modest member. She smiled at him as she shook the can of cream. If he'd been hung below as he was above, he undoubtedly would have been too arrogant to be allowed to live.

She began decorating her body with the cream, running pearls of it across her neck and making cream pasties for her breasts. She filled her navel, then decorated the cherry pie with the rest of the cream. "What a bad little puppy dog you are today."

"What?"

"Close your mouth. You're drooling." She took a fingerful of cream from the top of the pie and put it in her mouth, sucking it off slowly, never taking her eyes off him, even when she withdrew the finger, then licked the dark crimson nail with the tip of her pointed tongue. "On second thought, don't close your mouth. Just get over here. Now."

The professor of English, fresh out of words, did as she commanded, cleaning her neck first. Malory shivered with pleasure and glanced at the bedroom window as he moved to her breasts. On the open windowsill, a chipmunk watched, bright-eyed, as it nibbled a Peanut M&M. Malory blew it a kiss.

Ladies of the Lake

Ten

Hidden in forest shadows, crickets scraped their rhythmic mating calls. Night birds called to one another from fragrant pine boughs, and below, deer wandered the carpet of pine needles and the first fallen leaves of the season, nibbling still-growing grasses, tasting leaves. October nights in this hilly forest were colder than those on the coast, but no frosts ever came this early and even in the coldest part of winter, snow was a rarity. Applehead Forest, with its moderate climate and watchful elementals, was prime real estate for beasts and birds, as well as ghosts.

Applehead Lake lay calm under the light of the waning half-moon. As black and shining as polished onyx, it hid its secrets in cold-water silence, though if someone had taken a boat out and rowed into the still waters northwest of Applehead Island, they would have spied glowing amber jewels deep down. Unless they knew the stories, they would assume these were reflections of stars, because the human mind usually finds a way to make sense of things, even if that means ignoring the fact that the sense, when examined closely, makes no sense.

Tonight, a cobweb of ghost lights spread outward from the stained-glass church window at the center of the drowned town. Lights moved along long-gone roads, held by invisible hands, hung from hooks on phantom horse carts.

If a diver could descend undetected to observe the lights up close, he might have caught glimpses of spirits, flashes of long-dead humanity, living their afterlives among roofless, rotting buildings. He might have sensed undines moving among the human spirits, drawing sustenance from the water and the ghosts.

Some of the ghosts inhabiting the long-dead town of Applehead had been there for a century or more, some were new residents. All were prisoners, though few had the wit left to realize it. Most were nothing but afterthoughts, soulless supernatural energies captured when they drowned in these dark waters, but a few were true spirits, nearly all of them feminine, murdered, forever young, their bodies brought to the lake and personally interred within the old church by the queen of the Fata Morgana and her familiar.

If a human diver found his way into the building and knew where to look, he might even see the remains, the bones of the long dead and, if he looked in an old confessional-sized room, he might have spied the untouched bodies of two special young women. One was recently deceased, the other long dead, their beauty preserved somehow by the deep chilled water, their hair, blond and dark chestnut, waving in the currents. Though each had been weighted down and placed in different parts of the church, they were now entwined, like sisters comforting one another during a frightening thunderstorm.

That the perfect corpses had come together was a secret even from Malory Thomas; indeed Malory had never seen the unsullied body of the girl with chestnut curls, and simply assumed that it had turned into one of the nameless piles of bones whose owners were doomed to walk the submerged streets of Applehead for eternity. If she had known, she would have realized that the perfection had something to do with the spirit's ability to escape her watery tomb and torment her, for in all these years, despite many other sacrifices moldering here, Holly Gayle had been the only one able to walk on land.

Now there were two.

Blond hair and chestnut hair blended together in the gentle current. One dead hand seemed to caress the other's cheek, and if the imaginary diver saw the movement, after the initial shock, he would have assumed that the water currents were responsible for the action, because that was the only thing that made sense.

Eleven

Malory Thomas, still enjoying the aftereffects of serving Professor Tongue a few pieces of cherry pie, entered Gamma House with a serene smile on her face and Brittany hurrying along beside her, munching down sunflower seeds, shells and all.

"That was great!" the little blonde said for the tenth time since they had left Tongue's cottage. "Malory, what did you do to him?"

They passed the great room and parlor and walked into the kitchen. "I inspired him with a speech this afternoon," Malory said as she peered into the refrigerator. "I inspired an entire class."

"You did that old orgasm spell on your speech class?" Brittany giggled up the scales.

"Yes," Malory told her. She grabbed her private pitcher of unsweetened lemonade and an apple for Brittany, and brought them to the kitchen table where her bright-eyed familiar had stalled out and sprawled out on a wooden chair. Setting the items down as the little blonde dumped the last of her sunflower seeds into her mouth, Malory took a tall glass from the cupboard, retrieved some ice and a bottle of Absolut from the freezer, then sat down.

"I wish I'd been there," Brittany said before biting into the big green apple.

Malory poured sour lemonade over the ice, followed it with a big splash of vodka. "You would have turned feral and suffocated poor Professor Tongue, right there on his desk."

Chirrupy giggles tripped over the apple into the room. "You think so?"

"I know you, my little nut cruncher. I know you well."

Brittany held her apple out. "Look, Malory. A worm!"

"Half a worm."

She took another bite. "Worm's all gone."

"And you call yourself a vegetarian."

Brittany grinned. "It sure took you a long time to invite me into Tongue's bed tonight. I thought I was going to die of voyeurism."

"Can I help it if he's a slow eater?"

"Next time, take the stems off first. That'll speed him up."

"You know what they say, Britt. Patience is good for the soul." Malory topped off her half-finished drink with icy vodka.

"Who says *that?*"

"*They* do."

"Who's *they?*"

"Hi, guys." Heather Horner entered the room, pausing near the doorway. "Am I interrupting anything?"

"Who said patience is good for the soul?" Brittany chirped.

"Nobody. I forget what's good for the soul, but patience is a virtue."

Brittany stuck out her tongue at Malory. "You were wrong."

"And you have no virtue."

"Neither do you."

"Be good, or you won't get an invitation the next time I prime Professor Tongue for a marathon. How many orgasms did you have tonight, hmm?"

Brittany's musical chittering filled the room. "I don't know." She turned to Heather. "Do you count your orgasms?"

Heather smiled as she grabbed a glass and filled it with purple energy juice made by Mildred McArthur. She brought it to the table. "I usually have two or three. Once, I had five." She looked at the vodka. "May I, Malory?"

"You add liquor to your buzz juice?"

"Sure. Don't you?"

"Go ahead, but no. You know I don't drink that stuff."

"Why not?"

Because one of the ingredients is Brittany's urine. Why do you think it makes you so peppy? "For the same reason you don't drink my sour lemonade. I don't like it." Heather had been with them for over sixty years now, but that was a drop in the eternal bucket. She wasn't ready yet to know what was in her beloved purple juice. Or maybe she was, but it was more fun not to tell her.

"So, what's up, Heather?" Brittany asked.

"One of our new sisters has changed rooms without asking permission."

"Oh?" Malory considered. Maybe she was just feeling mellow from the evening workout, but the news didn't interest her much. "We do let them

choose their own rooms." *Third time's the charm.*
She topped her drink with Russian elixir once more.

"I know," Heather said. "I just thought you should
know. Merilynn has moved in with Kendra Phillips."

"Oh?" Malory stared into her drink. She rarely im-
bibed alcohol and already had a definite buzz on.
Getting a buzz was rarer than rare. "I didn't realize
they were friendly with one another."

"No, but now they're in there jabbering away like
long-lost sisters."

"They both like ghost stories," Brittany observed
while balancing the apple core on the tip of her nose.

"And there's the Eve Camlan connection," Malory
said.

"Kendra was her roommate, but what's the connection with Merilynn?"

"They went to Applehead Cheer Camp together,"
Malory snapped. "Gods, woman, you're the damned
head of the cheerleaders and you don't know that?"

"I remember now. Give me a break. Merilynn isn't
on the squad and Eve never said a word about her. It's
not exactly big news. It's not like I was a counselor at
that camp when they were there."

"Touchy," Brittany said, cocking her head to look
at Heather, proudly keeping the apple core precari-
ously balanced. "Why so touchy?"

"Just antsy. Sorry. You know what night it is, don't
you?"

"Thursday?" Malory said. She poured more lemon
juice, more Absolut. *Absolut sorcery.* She smiled
lazily. "Britt, you look like a trained seal. You want
some fish as a reward for your balancing act?"

"What else is today?" Heather added a little more
booze to her purple juice.

"Two weeks until All Hallows Eve? The day before Professor Piccolo shows up in class with his tongue in traction?" Her laugh was low and easy, her good mood still on the increase. Tonight, her sleep would be perfect. It could be nothing else. Tongue had wrung every orgasm out of her body, left her every cell depleted and her soul complete. Rarely had she ever been so satiated. "Who cares?"

"Oh, shit!" Brittany cried. The apple core fell and rolled across the linoleum.

"It's fifteen days until Halloween. It's the night of the October half-moon, duh!"

Malory regarded Heather. "I wish you wouldn't pick up so many of those tiresome expressions. 'Duh' isn't worthy of a Fata Morgana." She poured more booze.

"You yourself point out that we have to maintain current speech patterns," Heather said, her voice threaded with irritation. "What do you want me to say, 'It's the bee's knees?'"

"Bee's knees!" Brittany repeated happily. "I loved that line. Twenty-three skidoo. The queen's eyes! The butler's balls!" She looked at Malory. "Seriously, Mal, it is *the* night."

"I know. The anniversary of the flooding of Applehead. The ghosts down there are going crazy with their light show."

"A half-moon on this date means we might do some heavy banishing," Brittany reminded her. "It doesn't happen every year."

"There's something I don't understand," Heather said. Done with her purple juice, she poured two fingers of straight vodka in her glass.

"What?"

"Why do the ghosts under the lake act up on the anniversary of the flooding? The town was uninhabited. No one was killed."

"Don't be stupid," Malory drawled. "The spirit of the town is what lights up. It's nothing, just a ghost vision."

"What about your sacrifices?"

"Our sacrifices," Brittany corrected. "They're always there, right, Malory?"

"Right, especially that ridiculous dead twat Holly. They all seem to become active on the anniversary. I suppose they pick up on the energy of the phantom town." Reluctantly, she looked at Brittany. "You're right. We don't get a banishing night on the anniversary very often. Maybe we should convene and try to keep that little bitch under the lake where she belongs once and for all."

"You're slurring," Brittany observed. "You know what happens to your spells when you've been drinking."

Both of them burst into laughter.

"What?" Heather demanded, pouring another finger or two. "What happens?"

"You know," Malory said. "You were there once."

"Where once?"

"Here once."

"When you idiots got loaded and tried to cast a glamour on that soldier group," Brittany explained.

"The UFO show recruiter!" Malory said, flashing back to a World War II stint at Greenbriar.

"U *S* O!" Brittany got up and rifled through a cupboard until she found a can of mixed nuts. She pulled the tab, moaning slightly as the aroma escaped, then poured the delicacies into a bowl and returned to the table. Taking a handful for herself, she nudged the bowl toward the other two Fata Morganas. "Eat."

"You're *sharing?*" Malory teased. She winked at Heather. "She thinks we're drunk. She only shares when she's worried."

"Why are you worried?" Heather picked out some almonds for her very own.

"You don't remember the USO recruiter?"

"Bob Hope?"

Malory laughed. "You don't remember! You had to have been there."

Heather shook her head as she sucked on a nut. Brittany watched hungrily, even though her own cheeks were already fat with peanuts. "It was here?"

"Yes," Brittany said. "Are you ever going to chew that almond, or are you just going to tongue it to death?"

"She's going to tongue it till it climaxes," Malory mumbled. She put a Brazil nut on her long sharp tongue and pointed at it. Brittany smiled and leaned over, using her tongue to draw it into her own mouth.

She crunched. "Big nut."

Malory giggled. She heard herself and thought, *I don't giggle. It's too silly.* Then she giggled some more, realizing she was getting horny again, and put a pecan half on her tongue. Brittany went for it but Malory was quicker, drawing her tongue back, making her familiar go after it.

"Oh, Gods, don't you two ever get enough?" Heather asked, showing boredom. "Tell me about the USO guy."

Mistress and familiar drew apart. Malory, her mouth nutless, told Heather, "It was just a silly little spell. You remember, the guy was handsome and arrogant as hell? We decided to give him a tail?"

Heather laughed. "I wasn't there, I swear. Are you sure it was during that war? When else have you been here?"

"Vietnam," Brittany said. "Early seventies. *That's* when we did the glamour on the USO guy. Time flies, huh, Malory?"

"It does. Like little grains of sand, so fly the days of our lives."

"You're toasted," Heather told Malory.

"You and your slang."

"'Toasted' means smoking marijuana," Brittany said.

"It does?" Heather asked.

"I think so. I mean, it makes sense. Smoke, toast, it involves heat."

"Brittany's my guiding light," Malory said. *Gods, what a combination. Sex and alcohol. The Greeks really had things down pat.* "She stays with me as the world turns."

"You *are* fucked up!" Brittany giggled. She turned to Heather. "You weren't there?"

"Where were you in seventy-two?" Malory asked. A little part of her mind, the sober part, was bitching at her to get up, get it together, and go out and try to banish Holly Gayle, who no doubt was dragging her ectoplasmic ass out of the water as they sat here at the table sopping up modern mead. *The Greeks weren't so hot after all. They drank mead. Vodka beats the bee's knees out of mead.*

"In 1972," said Heather, "you had me running the Gamma Eta Pi chapter in Jeremy, Arizona."

Malory laughed. "Oh, I remember that. Jeremy, Arizona. You'd pissed me off. You did something . . ."

"She beat you into JFK's pants during that private party at the White House in 1961," Brittany said. "Malory, I expect humans to get stupid when they're drunk, but *you?*"

"Blame the Tongue. My defenses are toasted."

"That means—"

"Shut up, you little rodent. I know what it means. So, how *was* Jeremy, Arizona, Heather? Or did I ask you that already?"

"It was full of cock, Malory. I rode a lot of bucking broncos. In fact, I wouldn't mind going back to that little college out there again someday. Ever see a guy in chaps, no jeans?"

In response, Malory put another nut on her tongue and looked meaningfully at Brittany.

She took peanuts from the bowl and ate them, looking at Malory's invitation. "You need to get laid," she said. "You're getting too much oral sex. How long since you've ridden a Knight?"

"Too long. How about you, Heather?"

"Yesterday." She poured more vodka, for herself, then for Malory. "So, what's the skinny on Professor Tongue?"

"Never you mind," Malory said. "I don't share." She paused. "You get the best-hung Knight on the team into my bed, maybe I'll tell you a little."

"Maybe she'll let you watch," Brittany offered.

"Maybe," Malory agreed. "Now get your mind out of your vagina and tell Heather what you did to the USO guy."

Twelve

"I'm done," Kendra told her new roommate as she closed her notebook and set down her pen. "No more homework tonight. How about you?"

"Not a drop." Merilynn sat in a cross-legged yoga position on a small round hooked rug she'd placed on the floor near her bed. It was one of the less peculiar of her possessions, if you didn't count the fact that she'd made this rug herself and it depicted a nun and a satyr holding hands as they ran across a field of daisies. Now she stood up and stretched, twisting and turning and reaching for the sky. Then she sat on her bed, again crossing her legs so that her feet looked trapped.

"How do you do that?" Kendra asked.

Merilynn grinned. "Watch this." She untied her legs, parting them and putting the soles of her feet together. Then she tugged her ankles forward until her knees stuck out almost even with her hips.

"Ouch!" Kendra grimaced. "Are you double-jointed?"

"No. I just bend this way. I couldn't do those cheerleader splits to save my soul . . . Sorry, that came out wrong."

Kendra smiled softly. "It's okay. I'm glad you're here, and I'm glad you brought your stuff."

"You like?" Merilynn gestured at the stars-and-moon bedspread she sat on; the flowery one that Eve loved had been returned to Gamma's linen closet.

"I love it. It makes the room happier. It's different. You don't happen to have some funky curtains so we can get rid of those ruffly white things, do you?"

"I'll ask Father to bring some when he comes to visit. I have ones that match my bedspread."

"I love that spread. The brilliant blues and golds are way more my speed than this floral pastel stuff."

"In my room, I had twin beds. There's another spread. Shall I ask him to bring the other one for you?"

Kendra barely hesitated. "Yes! So, did you bring any art for the walls?"

"I have a couple watercolors in a folio I stuck in my closet. They're scenery. I don't know if you'd like them or not."

Kendra nodded toward a small framed print of geese with bonnets that had come with the room. "That's sure not what I like. Let me see."

"Okay."

It took Merilynn about ten seconds to get to the closet and pull out her folio. She opened it and took out a medium-sized watercolor of a forest lake at night.

"That's Applehead Lake." Kendra stood up and moved closer. "It's spooky."

"I didn't think you'd like it," Merilynn said, starting to put it away.

"No, I do like it. It's spooky. Spooky's good."

"You're weird," Merilynn said warmly. "I like you."

Kendra continued to study the painting. It was dark, full of greens and blues, the black lake water reflecting the full moon above. "We have to get a frame and put it up."

"I have poster frames." Merilynn set the painting down and lifted another. "Déjà vu, almost," she announced as she lifted it up.

It was the lake at night again, much like the other painting, but here the view was from the water, not the shore, and the moon was half and partly obscured by clouds. A thin mist hovered on Applehead Island. There was an additional sparkle to the lake. Kendra looked closer. "You've painted in the ghost lights."

"When I saw them, I tried to memorize them so I could draw them. The first time, I drew them in crayon as soon as I got home. There must be a hundred versions of this painting at home. This is the best one."

"Do you take art classes?"

"One now, but it's just a hobby. I took art in high school and the teacher specialized in watercolors. She taught me the tricks, you know, how to do water and light."

"What's that?" Kendra asked. "It looks like a stained-glass window." She paused, looking at the artist. "You said you saw this once?"

Merilynn nodded.

"You saw the window?"

Another nod. "You know about the window?"

Now Kendra nodded. "It's up in the administration building's tower. Are you sure it's the same window?"

Merilynn laughed lightly. "It was way too deep to see details. I like to think it is, though. That's how the story goes, after all."

"I would kill to see it. All of it. The lights."

Merilynn put the painting back in the folio, looking pleased. "You believe me?"

"Why not? I mean, I don't know what it is, but I

believe you saw it. Folklore usually has roots in something real, don't you think?"

"Yes. Absolutely." She pulled a much smaller painting from the folio, not showing it to Kendra. "This one, you won't want on the wall."

"Let me be the judge of that."

"I don't want it on the wall."

"You painted it and you don't want it up? Is it terrible?"

"No. It's pretty good, if I say so myself. But if you thought the lake pictures were spooky, well, then this is spooky to the tenth power."

"Show me, already!"

Merilynn slowly turned the painting and as she saw it, Kendra's flesh rose in goose bumps. It was a watercolor of a woman's pale face and dark eyes staring up from just beneath the water. She was frightening to look at, eerie, but as she studied her, Kendra discerned a look of pleading in her eyes, not anger, not terror, but sadness and longing. "Holly."

"Yes."

"She's beautiful. So sad."

"She wants something," Merilynn said.

"What?"

"To be found, I think. That night, she almost dragged Sam under. It was like she hypnotized her. I pulled her back—you can't repeat any of this to her."

Kendra nodded. "I remember, you said that before."

A pixie grin. "Can't be too careful!"

"Hypnotizing her . . . That doesn't sound very friendly."

"No, it doesn't, but I'm not sure it means she's wicked or anything. I think she's desperate."

"Sam Penrose doesn't seem like the kind of person

who would let herself be hypnotized," Kendra said, wanting to slow things down.

"I agree. She's not now and she wasn't then. But it happened."

"Can we get her to talk about it, do you think?"

Merilynn shrugged. "I'm not sure. You can't tell her I told you anything; sorry, I said it again."

"That's okay. You're worried. Go on."

"We could invite her over for pizza or something. I can talk about what I saw, maybe she'd talk, but don't count on it. Maybe we could start by getting her talking about camp. The adventures. If you let her know you believe in ghosts, she might open up more."

"Let's do it, but not here," Kendra said, unconsciously lowering her voice.

"Okay, but why not?"

"I'm paranoid."

"Yes, well, I can understand that. But we're just telling old kid stories. Who cares if anyone hears?"

"I don't know, but I have a feeling someone might. I think we should be careful."

"If that's how you feel."

"I do."

"Then we should be careful." Merilynn set the portfolio aside. "Kendra? Why do you believe in ghosts?"

"My granny says she saw one and I believe her," Kendra began. "Other women in my family saw them. Perfectly intelligent people see things that can't be explained."

"But why do *you* believe?"

"Why not? I think they're memories and sometimes we can see or hear or smell them." She shivered, remembering Eve's telling of her nightmare shortly before her death. "They come in dreams, conjured up by our minds most of the time, but sometimes they come from outside us. Sometimes they're real. I used to think that ghosts were just mindless shadows drifting around, but maybe some of them can think. Maybe there are actual *spirits* out there once in a while." She stood up and closed the double-hung window over her desk without looking out.

"You've seen one." It was a statement, not a question.

Kendra turned to face Merilynn. "Yes."

"Holly?"

"No." She walked to Merilynn's bed and sat next to her, then bent to her ear and whispered, "I saw Eve."

Merilynn's eyes opened wide and she mouthed one word: *When?*

"After the initiation. That night. It was near dawn."

"We were drugged."

"I know, I know. I've tried to convince myself it was a hallucination, but it wasn't. I wish it were. I *know* she was real. She came to tell me something."

"What?"

Kendra shook her head. "I don't remember. I keep trying, but I just can't figure out what it was. Sometimes I think she asked for help, but like you said, they'd drugged us, so I don't trust my memory."

Merilynn laid her hand over Kendra's. "Let's talk more later. Want to go out for a pizza? If you want, we can invite Sam."

Kendra glanced at her watch. It was barely after eight and all she'd had for dinner was a cup of instant soup. Her stomach growled so loudly that Merilynn could hear it.

"I'll take that as a yes."

They stood and got their bags and shrugged into

their jackets. "Are you a vegan?" Kendra asked as Merilynn paused to tuck the paintings into her closet.

"No. Why?"

"You look like a vegan."

"Gee, thanks. What does a vegan look like?"

"Sorry. I mean, you do the yoga thing and the herb thing. It just kind of seemed to go together."

"Think again. I like my steaks medium rare and my carrots completely cooked. Or completely raw." They left the room and pulled the door closed behind them.

"I hate not having a lock," Kendra said.

"Me too." They walked a short way toward the staircase and stopped at Sam Penrose's door. Merilynn knocked. "Sam? Are you in there?"

"Who is it?"

"Merilynn and Kendra. Are you busy?"

Sam opened the door and looked them up and down. "I'm always busy. Why?"

"We're going for pizza. You want to come?"

Sam glanced back toward her desk, then nodded. "I'm never too busy for pizza." She eyed the pair again. "You two aren't vegans or anything like that, are you?"

"Pepperoni," said Kendra.

"Sausage," said Merilynn.

"And onions," Sam said. "Let me get my coat." She left the door open while she put her computer to sleep and fiddled around.

Merilynn looked at Kendra. "Do you know what tonight is?"

"Thursday?"

"It's the anniversary of the day they flooded out the town of Applehead."

"Oh, heavens, you're right." Kendra smiled. "I should have known that. Granny always said the town comes to life on the day it drowned."

"Yeah." Merilynn's eyes lit up. "When the town lights up, Holly Gayle walks."

"What are you two giggling about?" Sam demanded, joining them.

"Nothing," Merilynn said.

"History," Kendra said simultaneously.

"Funny history? You'll have to tell me all about it while we go into town."

"I thought we'd just go to the cafeteria," Merilynn said.

Sam pulled car keys from her jacket pocket. "You call that mush they serve there pizza? It's a pancake with some tomato sauce smeared on it. If we're going to eat pizza, we're going to do it right."

"It's a weeknight," Kendra said. "Caledonia's pretty far. I don't want to be dead in the morning. Dead tired, I mean."

They started down the grand staircase. "What else would you mean?" Sam asked, her tone teasing. "I found a pizza place in Greenbriar. It's not great, except compared to school food. Then it's sublime."

"Let's go!" Kendra said, her stomach echoing her desire.

Thirteen

"The USO guy," Malory said, "wasn't that big of a deal. He was hanging around campus, supposedly looking to discover new talent to take on military show tours. Brit, do you remember his name? Something like Dick Biggs?"

"Peter Long." Brittany giggled.

Heather went to the fridge and found a jug of orange juice. "So what did you do to him?" she asked, sitting down and pouring until her glass was two-thirds full. She added vodka.

"You are going to be sick tomorrow," Malory observed.

"And you're not?"

"I'm not like you. I'm immune to such petty annoyances as hangovers."

"Oh." Heather looked at her glass dubiously. "Can you do a spell to keep me from getting a hangover?"

Brittany cackled with amusement. "Never ask her to do a spell when she's like this. You'll know why in a minute. Tell her what you did, Malory."

Malory decided to sulk and put a fresh peanut on her tongue. Brittany gave her a long-suffering look, then leaned forward and nabbed it with her mouth.

"Ouch! You little bitch, you bit me."

"You needed biting, Mistress. Now, tell her what you did."

"Well, Captain Long—I don't remember if he was a captain, but I liked the sound of it so I called him that—he was a work of art. Chiseled chin with a cleft on a square jaw. One of those blond Nordic warrior types with eyes the color of a clear summer sky." She chuckled. "I'm a poet. Anyway, he knew how good he looked. He had broad shoulders and a six-pack."

"Of beer?" Heather asked.

"Abs," Brittany said.

"One night, the last night he was here, he came to Gamma House. He wanted the cheerleaders to give him an impromptu performance. He said he was thinking of taking them on the tour.

"They did it. That year none of them were Fata Morganas, just Gammas, and they made fools of themselves, falling all over each other, completely in heat. Captain Long had looks and an aura of charisma and sexuality that were really quite interesting." She poured another drink. "Heather, I want to ride a Knight tonight. Make that happen."

"Malory, Heather's going to be lucky to make it upstairs to her own bed," Brittany said.

"Whatever. Then you get me a Knight, Brittany."

"Tell your story first."

"Okay. Captain Long was an ass. I knew it the moment I met him, but he kept it well hidden. He was in the parlor with the squad. One man, eight girls. It was a warm night, not long before school would be out for the summer, and he kept encouraging the girls to remove garments."

"Were they wearing their uniforms?"

"No, no. This was impromptu. I remember lots of

bell-bottom jeans and tie-dyed shirts. It was the Age of Aquarius." She paused and started to sing, "This is the dawning of—"

"Tell the story," Brittany ordered, "before Heather passes out."

"Right. Do you know that my mentor, when I was a young girl, before I found immortality, he predicted an Age of Aquarius?" Brittany rolled her eyes, so Malory got back on track. Britt was a pain, but as a familiar she was great at keeping her organized.

"I'm an Aquarius," Heather slurred.

"That's nice," Malory said. "I was born—when was I born, Brittany?"

"You're older than dirt," Brittany said. She rose and went for the jug of purple juice. It would bring Heather back to earth, at least a little.

"Hey! You can't talk to me that way! I'll turn you into a—a rectum!"

Brittany grabbed a fresh glass and patted Malory's head as she returned. "Not just any old rectum, I hope," she said, pouring purple juice. "Here, Heather, drink up—no, no booze. This will wake you up."

"I want more vodka."

"After you drink this." Brittany sat. "So Captain Long was getting the squad to undress."

Malory nodded. "I'd cloaked myself in an invisibility spell so no one would notice me and I sat right there, taking it all in."

"And drinking," Brittany added. "Drinking tequila sunrises. That was the in drink back then. Jimmy Buffet sang about them all the time."

"They were good."

"Your drink was cloaked too?" Heather asked.

She'd had half the purple juice and was sharper already.

"Hey, I'm not just any old Sybil, you know. I could have cloaked a roast chicken and eaten it and they wouldn't have known."

"As long as she didn't burp." Brittany giggled. She started in on the bowl of nuts again.

"You whore," Malory said affectionately. "I ought to tie you down and—"

"You were watching the girls and Captain Long," Brittany said. "Was he undressing too?"

"Not yet. He sweet-talked those girls into taking off every iota of clothing. They were drinking too."

"Tequila sunrises," Brittany said.

"Mostly. And Captain Long, he just had a bottle of tequila he was nursing. A bottle and a lime and a salt shaker. It was mescal, the liquor, I mean, the kind with the worm in it, and there wasn't a lot there. He had no intention of getting so drunk he couldn't get it up. It was nauseating to watch. He kept showing the Gammas the worm and threatening to eat it."

"Swallow it," Brittany corrected.

"Oh, how do you know, you little slut? Maybe he was going to chew it up!"

"He was an ass, not a moron."

Malory decided not to push it. She needed some tail and someone to supply it. *Best to keep Brittany smiling.* "I was amazed. The man didn't have a magical bone in his body, but between the charm and the booze, he'd gotten every last one of them to take off their clothes. And then he had them undress him. One item of clothing per girl. They had to use their teeth. Why, he had them all over him, biting his buttons, yanking his belt, unzipping. They were in his thrall. That night, the tequila hit me. It doesn't often, you know. I'm not susceptible ordinarily."

"The story. You were drunk, they were undressing him. Then what happened?"

"I was really starting to get pissed off," Malory admitted. "Those were *my* girls, my handpicked little Gamma sisters, and he was manipulating them! That's *my* job!"

"I know, Mistress. Go on."

Sweet Brittany. Malory loved it when she called her that in front of other sisters. She rarely did it. "Well, then, once he was stripped naked, he stood up and I nearly dropped my drink. He was perfect. Absolutely perfect. I thought of commandeering him for myself. But then he opened his mouth and he commanded—*commanded*—*my* girls to perform fellatio on him. On their *knees.* He had them kneel in a line like they were worshipping the Forest Knight himself, and he began to go from one to another, *bathing* himself in *my girls'* mouths! If I hadn't been so horny, I would have flayed him, then and there."

"Did he have a big cock?" Heather giggled.

"It was a fine specimen," Malory said, the fire in her belly growing stronger. "Fearsomely rampant, so hard you could have hung a coat on it and it would have stayed up."

"What kind of coat?"

"Be quiet, Brittany."

"You can tell a lot about a man by the weight of the coat he wears." The familiar giggled.

Malory pulled the dish of nuts to herself.

"Hey!"

"Apologize."

"I apologize. Now, let me have my nuts."

Malory smiled and pushed them back over to Brittany. "I watched, furious, as my girls obeyed his orders. Finally, I left the room and removed the spell, then walked back in and gave them hell. The cheerleaders were humiliated and ran off shrieking, grabbing their clothes. That was the whoriest bunch of cheerleaders we ever had—"

"Hey," Heather said, back into the vodka again, "my squad isn't slutty."

"Shhh. That wasn't your squad." Brittany pushed the vodka bottle out of Heather's reach. "They were total skanks. But it was the era. Free love. They liked to paint each other in body paint and do cheers. Once—"

"*I'm* telling the stories here!" Malory interrupted. The room was starting to spin a little, so she poured sour lemonade to drink without the booze. "After they ran off, Captain Long just stood there, smiling at me, naked as the day he was born."

"What happened to the coat?" Heather asked.

"What coat?"

"The one on his cock."

"You're an idiot. There was no coat. He was naked. He actually said to me, 'Do you like what you see?' The arrogance of the man was astonishing. Then it got worse. He said, 'You didn't have to send them off. There's enough of me to go around.' He wanted me to call them back so that he could share his magnificent body with *all* of us! That bastard had no intention of giving us any pleasure. He just wanted to *be* pleasured."

"So what did you do?"

"I walked up to him and grabbed his penis. He loved it. He said, 'You want me.' Well, if there was any desire left in me, that killed it completely. I'd been torn before, thinking I'd ride him and see if he was good enough to spare. I thought maybe I'd cast a glamour and give him a tail or turn him into a sex slave for the Fata Morganas. But that was too much. I cast a different glamour. I tried, but I was drunk and it didn't work quite the way I planned."

"Tell me!" Heather squealed.

Malory smiled. "Well, I decided to shorten his penis to a nub that would make Professor Tongue look like a stud. I knew something would happen when I did, it always does, doesn't it, Brittany?"

"It does."

"What do you mean?"

"When you re-form humans, every action causes a reaction of some sort. When I took away his nice big penis, something else on him would grow. I'd done it in years past and it often resulted in long earlobes or nipples, or even a foot-long scrotum. But not this time. The alcohol made me twist something in the spell and his penis grew longer and longer, like Pinnochio's nose. Nothing else changed on him, because it was simply a re-formation of its own mass. It became as slender as my finger and fell past his knees. He just stood there, not believing what he saw."

"And you?" Heather asked. "What did you think?"

"I just laughed. I laughed until Brittany showed up."

"I laughed too. It was like he had this long tube hanging down. You should have seen it. Then Mallory picked up his bottle of tequila."

"What was he doing?"

"Nothing," Malory said. "The man was a statue. He was utterly shocked."

"Malory picked up the tequila," Brittany repeated,

"and pointed at the worm floating in it. I knew instantly what she was thinking."

"Of course you did," Malory cooed, thinking about sex again. "You're my little monkey."

"Never call me a monkey. That's degrading. I'd never be a monkey, not even for you!"

"Sorry, little one." She looked at Heather. "Together, Brittany and I cast a major glamour on Captain Long's very long, thin penis."

"We turned it into a worm." Brittany giggled.

"And the worm turned," Malory finished. She drained her juice and started to stand up.

"Wait a minute!" Heather cried. "What does that mean? What happened? You really turned his cock into a worm?"

"A fat white worm. Fat for a worm, not for a penis," Malory said. "The kind in the tequila, with little catepillar legs. Thousands of them."

"It crawled up Captain Long and wrapped itself around his neck. He was strangled by his own dick!" Brittany finished.

"Was that part of the spell?"

Malory shrugged. "I'm horny. Let's go find some Knights. I want to joust with one or two. Ladies?"

"What did you do with the body?" Heather asked. Fortified by the secret ingredients in the purple juice, she was smashed yet ambulatory, and managed to stand up with the others.

"In the lake," Malory said.

"So he's walking tonight? His spirit is trapped?"

"Yes, Heather. I thought you had that all figured out. The spirits of those we kill and dump in the lake stay in the lake for all time."

"What if you don't dump them in the lake?"

"Then they either wander the area, or we banish them. Remember, dear, we banished Mulva's spirit after we got rid of her in the forest? I wouldn't want a traitorous bitch like her hanging around, would you?"

"No. But why does Holly escape the lake? Why only her? None of the others?"

Malory regarded Heather with hooded eyes. "I don't know. A power she possesses, some sort of magic of her own."

"And you've tried to banish her?"

Irritated, Malory pushed her chair in and adjusted her shirt. "Yes, Heather, we've tried. And yes, we should try again tonight, but I'd rather get laid." She traded looks with her familiar, who was as aware as she was that banishing Holly Gayle was so difficult, not because Holly had powers of her own, but because it was just possible she had stolen a power of Malory's.

It was something that only she and Brittany knew about and suspected. *The stone.* Malory's powerful emerald, set in the haft of a small silver dagger, had been lost the night they killed Holly Gayle. *Lost or stolen.* The stone, a gift from the Forest Knight long, long ago, when her brother was still alive, had pulsed with power, glowing green like the eyes of the knight himself. It was a key to her true strength; without it she was powerful in her own right; with it she was invincible. She and Brittany had spent years searching for it, returning to Greenbriar more often than they should, searching the woods, placating the Forest Knight with sacrifices, far more of them than he had demanded when the stone had given her more solid immortality. When she wasn't so in his debt.

The knight had not forgiven the loss or theft of the

stone, and would not until she found it again. Until then, she would have to beg with extra sacrifices, to keep her youth. Until then, she would continue to search the woods and the tunnels below Applehead Island and the old, dead town. She had even gone into the water, into the old church, looking, but so far had found nothing.

Lust and longing grew in her heart at the thought of it. "Maybe," she said softly, "we should go into the woods tonight."

"What for?" Heather asked, oblivious of her mood. "I thought you wanted to get laid."

Malory glanced at her, nodding slightly. There was power in that as well. *You are drunk! Don't be foolish!* "Okay, let's get laid," she said. "Then maybe we'll walk in the woods."

Fourteen

Greenbriar Pizza's pizza was about on par with a halfway decent frozen pie, but Merilynn wolfed her pieces down. Seeing she was a slice ahead of Sam and Kendra, she forced herself to slow down. She looked around. "This place is really something," she remarked as she plucked an olive from her new slice and ate it slowly.

"It is," Kendra said. "How did you ever find it?"

Sam smiled. "I looked behind a newspaper rack and, voilà, there it was. Hiding." She reached for a new piece, picking one from the half that had mushrooms along with olives, onions, pepperoni, and red bell peppers.

Merilynn and Kendra had wanted sausage too, but Sam had nixed the idea, declaring it too likely to cause food poisoning. Like a good reporter, she built up a case in about fifteen seconds that neither of them could argue with. Sausage, after all, was always iffy. And in this place . . .

Merilynn gazed at the decor of the long, skinny restaurant. It was primarily a take-out joint, but tables and chairs lined one side of the corridor that led back to the rest rooms. The lighting was low, with little red glass candle holders that held electric lights on each

Formica table, and the walls had posters of anything and everything Italian that the management could scavenge. There was a map of the country, travel posters of ruins, a bad painting of a vineyard, a horrendous painting of a man who might have faintly resembled the Godfather if the artist had been more talented. He wore a red-and-white-checked napkin tucked into his collar and stared at a pizza on a table—with a red-and-white-checked tablecloth, of course—before him, an expression that was supposed to be pleasure, but looked more like a gas attack, adorning his face. And no wonder. The high-piled pizza looked as if it were slathered with Play-Doh vegetables and blood. Merilynn nodded at it. "That's a real appetite inducer."

Kendra laughed. "Is that supposed to be Frank Sinatra?"

"I thought it was Marlon Brando," Merilynn said. *"The Godfather."*

"It looks more like John Belushi's last supper," Sam said.

"That's terrible!" Merilynn said. "It's mean." Then she laughed. "But I see the resemblance."

"Really, that's supposed to be Belushi," Sam said. "The owner says he ate here once. It's their claim to fame."

"I guess he didn't pose for the painting," Kendra said.

"The painting was done by the owner's wife. Don't let them hear you dissing it," Sam warned. "He thinks she's a Picasso."

"He's right," Kendra said softly. "Belushi's eyes aren't quite even. And one ear is higher than the other."

"Shhh. When I ordered, I told them I work for the

school paper," Sam said quietly. "We'll probably get a discount if you two don't blow it."

"But we already paid."

"Next time. After I write a nice review."

"Oh." Merilynn liked knowing Sam was planning ahead.

"Now," said the journalist sitting across from her and Kendra, "don't make a sound when you see it, but look at the painting hanging behind you, over the next table down."

They turned. The table was occupied by a couple of jocks from school, so their glance at the painting was blessedly brief. When she looked at Sam again, Merilynn was amused by the grin.

"What do you think?" Sam asked.

"Somebody threw up on the canvas?" Kendra asked.

"Come on, you *did* see it, didn't you?" Merilynn chided softly.

"Yes, I saw it," Kendra admitted. "But do those two guys sitting under it realize what's in it?"

"Probably not," Sam said. "It's for the best."

All three giggled. Merilynn tried to steal another glance, but caught the eye of Frank Steiner, the beefy wrestler from the speech class she and Sam were both in.

He grinned. "Hi, girls."

"Uh, hi." Merilynn spoke without enthusiasm. Beefy Boy was an oversexed tub of lard, his aura all disgusting, dirty red with lust, yellowish green with gluttony. The boy was a walking advertisement for several Deadly Sins.

"Hi," said the other guy. He was pudgy-husky. Another wrestler, probably.

Merilynn didn't recognize him, but Sam did. "Hi, Norton."

"Aren't you going to introduce me to your friends?" he asked.

Ewwww. Merilynn thought he was almost creepier than Frank Steiner. She didn't sense as lecherous an aura, but it was peculiar and prickly. He looked like a nerd. And sure enough—

"Merilynn, Kendra, this is Norton Simms. He's a computer systems major."

"And a wrestler!" he added. "I just made second string."

"How nice for you," Kendra said.

"Norton writes the computer column for the paper," Sam said dryly.

"Viruses are my specialty," Norton said.

"Giving them?" Merilynn asked, very turned-off.

"Are you flirting with my man, Merilynn?" Frank asked.

Merilynn rolled her eyes and turned her back on the pair. Kendra did the same.

"Hey, girls, want to join us?" Frank called.

"No," Sam said.

"Ah, come on. We have beer."

"We don't want any beer," Kendra replied. "School night."

"Who cares?" came Norton's voice. "Skip a class. Live a little."

The girls ignored them. Then Frank leaned his chair back, hot garlicky breath oozing over Merilynn's neck. "You're really cute," he said. "I love redheads."

"So, you mean you two aren't gay?" Sam asked, even more dryly, if it was possible.

"What?" Steiner and Simms squawked simultaneously.

"I thought you were a couple," Sam said matter-of-factly.

"If we're a couple because we're sitting together, then you three are pussy-licking dykes," Steiner snarled.

"Homophobe," Merilynn said softly to her friends.

"Did you call me a homo?" Steiner asked, turning uglier.

Merilynn turned and fixed him with her eyes. He flinched and looked away, but as soon as she turned back to her food, he was leaving stench on her neck again. "Why don't you let me show you just how much I like chicks?"

She ignored him.

Norton Simms spoke up, showing slightly more intelligence. *Slightly.* "Why did you say that about us? Because we're wrestlers?"

"Not at all," Sam replied nonchalantly. "It's because you chose to sit together at *that* table."

"This table?" Norton asked. "What's wrong with this table?"

Merilynn could feel ill will pouring off Steiner, even though he'd sat back up and was stuffing his face—you couldn't miss the sounds of his chewing. Like a wolf tearing up a deer.

"There's nothing wrong with the table," Sam said. "I thought you chose it because you found the painting above it titillating."

Merilynn and Kendra turned in time to see the boys look up at the antimasterpiece of art on the wall. Merilynn clapped her hand over her mouth to keep in her laughter as the wrestlers realized what they were sitting under.

It was a painting of the statue of David, in brilliant shades of pinkish flesh and no fig leaf. The owner's wife obviously thought highly of David's prowess. The statue showed a David who might have been posing on a very cold day. This David wasn't nearly so unhung. This David could be in a porno movie if he wanted.

"Shit!" said Steiner. He picked up the pizza platter and his mug. "Come on, we're moving away from these dykes. Get the pitcher."

The pair moved down to the table with the map of Italy over it, and the girls laughed so hard it hurt. "Shh," Sam said when she caught her breath. "Not so loud. We have classes with those guys."

"Samantha Penrose," Merilynn said, doffing an imaginary hat, "I salute you."

"Me too." Kendra started on another slice as she spoke. "So, you and Merilynn went to cheerleading camp together?"

Sam rolled her eyes. "That was a long time ago."

"Neither of you seem the type."

"Lord, no," Merilynn said. "I went for the ghost stories. What did you go for, Sam?"

"My parents wanted me to, and I decided to go ahead and do it so that I could write an exposé on cheerleaders."

"Come on," Kendra said. "An exposé? What were you, ten?"

"About that." Sam paused, pizza at her lips. "Why is that so hard to believe?"

"Ten-year-olds play with dolls and—"

"I had a doll once," Sam said tonelessly. "It talked. So I took it apart to see how it worked."

"You must have driven your poor mother crazy," Kendra said, smiling.

Sam's lips crooked up a little. "Probably." She sounded proud.

"That was the only doll you ever had?" Merilynn asked.

"Of course not. That was the last one. I don't remember when I was very small. I'm human, though. I probably played with them."

"You sound disgusted at the idea."

Sam shrugged and chewed, had a Pepsi chaser. "I was a tomboy."

"Not me," Merilynn said. "I loved dolls. I had Barbie and Ken. A couple of each."

"Me too," Kendra said. "They were fun for a while."

"Did you play games with them?" Merilynn asked.

"What do you mean? I guess I did the usual, you know, dressing them up and having little weddings, junk like that. Once I stuck a Ping-Pong ball under Barbie's dress and pretended she was pregnant. My granny thought that was rude." She laughed. "Is that what you mean?"

Merilynn trilled a laugh. "I took it a little further. Father's housekeeper—she lived in—she loved to sew. She made me Barbie and Ken costumes. I had an outfit for Ken that made him look like *The Exorcist*. You know, the priest costume, a black overcoat. She even made a little bag out of felt. So I'd dress him up as Father Damien—I had such a crush on that man, isn't that awful?—and I'd put makeup on Barbie. Not real makeup, but like I'd paint toothpaste on her face to make her look white and rub cayenne pepper on her eyes to make them look red."

Sam laughed so hard she launched a nugget of pizza. "Sorry. Cayenne pepper? I love it!"

"The housekeeper didn't wear makeup, so there wasn't any. Necessity's the mother of invention."

"I'll say."

"So, I'd put Barbie in her nightgown and tie her to her little Barbie bed and play *Exorcist.*" She paused. "I ruined a couple of them that way, but Father finally bought me one that bent better."

"He knew what you were doing?"

"Yes. Mostly. He's very open-minded. Heck, I was exorcising evil, how could he disapprove?"

"He let you see the movie that young?" Kendra asked.

"Yes." She cocked her head. "Is that weird?"

"I don't know. My mother and Granny would never let me see things like that. I think that would have given me nightmares, so I'm glad I didn't see it that young."

"Father always explained everything when I wanted to see something scary or weird. He always stayed with me and gave me the remote so I could turn off the VCR if I got freaked out. It was cool. Anyway, he did get mad once and took away my *Exorcist* costume."

"Why?" Sam asked.

"Well, he walked in while I was doing the crucifix scene, you know, where Regan screws herself with the cross?"

"And he disapproved?" Sam's eyebrow Spocked up, her mouth crooked with amusement.

"I was using the cross on his rosary beads. He never would have caught me though if I hadn't gotten so carried away."

"What do you mean?" Kendra asked.

"I was good at doing the possessed-Regan voice and right before he came in, I was saying, 'Fuck me! Fuck me!' just like in the movie."

"So he really came to bawl you out for saying fuck?" Sam said.

"Not bawl me out, but yes, that's what alerted him."

"He didn't bawl you out?" Kendra asked. "I would've gotten a mouthful of soap for saying that!"

"Father's realistic. He'd explain to me that the word was bad and I'd get in trouble for using it." She paused to chew. "That was good, because if he'd stuck soap in my mouth, I would have rebelled and started saying it every five seconds."

"What did you do after he took away your *Exorcist* costume?" Sam asked.

"He gave it back, but I'd made up lots of other games. I had nun costumes for all my Barbies. Old-fashioned costumes. So I liked to put one on Ken and one on Barbie."

"On *Ken?*" Sam asked, grinning.

"Well, he had his priest costume on underneath. I hardly ever made him into a transvestite. Usually, I pretended he was wearing it so that he could get into the nunnery and fool around with the nuns."

"Oh," Sam said wryly. "That's okay then."

"Goose," Merilynn said. "You're being silly."

"Did you ever play ghosts with them?" Kendra asked.

"Did I ever!"

Fifteen

The Pi Eta Gamma fraternity house was two stories of Federalist mansion, brick and stone, with a narrow pillared porch running across the front. There was none of the gracefulness of the Gamma's antebellum mansion; rather, it stood sharp and proud in true masculine fashion. Located ten minutes away (on foot), backed up to another part of the forest bordering the college property, it was the House of Jocks, and Malory was out to locate some, the bigger the better. One could only ride Professor Tongue so long before a good rooting became necessary.

Brittany and Heather and Michele, a Gamma officer, cheerleader, and Fata Morgana they'd met up with in the foyer on the way out, were with her. Michele carried a sixer of Michelob, and was killing one as they walked in order to catch up with her inebriated buddies.

Brittany, of course, never drank, but she didn't need to; she seemed to be in a perpetual state of intoxication. *Seemed* being the key word. That was how she liked to be perceived, a little goofy. Even Malory, who knew better, usually fell under the spell and underestimated her.

They entered the house, quietly pushing open one

of the unlocked tall green double-entry doors. It wasn't late, only nine-ish, and Brittany found the girls' stealth—including Malory's—amusing. It was the alcohol. It had them, for the moment, in sneaky mode. It pleased them, Brittany knew, because it made them feel wicked in an alcohol-silly sort of way. She watched her mistress. They had spent centuries together. Malory Thomas was a stone-cold killer, but right now she was as giggly as a little girl. Brittany liked that.

She also liked that she was after men tonight. While they were at the kitchen table, she had thought Malory was going to want to use her as a sex toy tonight—which wasn't bad, but it was exhausting, especially after the workout at the professor's. In fact, Brittany was still sated and thought that Malory ought to be as well. It wasn't like her, but then it wasn't like her to drink so much either. *The half-moon. The anniversary. She's nervous. She's avoiding the ghosts. Why?*

They walked down a corridor into the big main living room, and Brittany watched her mistress, growing more ill at ease with each passing moment. Malory was fearless. Always fearless—and with good reason. Tonight, there was a vulnerability. Maybe it was just the alcohol playing tricks. Maybe she truly hadn't thought about the anniversary and the activity in the lake tonight. About Holly Gayle's likeliness to appear on the grounds or in Gamma House.

But that rang false to Brittany too. Malory had spent the day having sex, going at it like a machine, insatiable. In her gut, Brittany believed she was avoiding something. *Holly.* But why? They'd seen her

many, many times over the years. Malory didn't fear
her; she usually thought of her as an annoying gnat.
When Holly had shown up and helped Eve Camlan
escape her fate, Malory was furious, not frightened.
But she's had time to think about it. That must be it.

"Hello, boys," Malory said, approaching some football players who were having a study group at a table
near the sofas and chairs. As at Gamma, the furniture
they favored was near the fireplace. Tonight, a chill
was in the air and they'd lit a fire. It crackled merrily
as it licked the logs and made Brittany wish to be at a
bonfire in the woods, to commune with the Forest
Knight, not these human boys. But what Malory
wanted, Malory got.

"Ladies!" Art Caliburn stood up and grinned.
Spence Lake, Duane Hieman, and Perry Seville did
the same. All varsity boys, all big and reasonably
handsome. Perry was smaller and more earnest than
the others, and Brittany decided he was the one for
her with his haunted blue eyes and black hair. He had
a look of innocence, and real or not, she liked that.

"Hi, Perry," she said, claiming her territory.
"Studying hard?"

"Hardly studying," he said, a little shy.

"We were just about to take a break," Duane said.
He was a big man of African descent. He had a warrior look about him, and Michele eyed him.

"We're tired of studying," she said. "Do you want
to do something, Duane?"

He looked surprised. "Sure."

Heather said, "Art?"

Malory cut in. "Art? Would you like to take me for
a walk?"

Heather glared; then the captain of the team did

something that Malory hated. He said, "Did you want to take a walk, Heather?" He looked at Malory while Heather stood there, obviously wanting to say yes, not daring to. "Malory, Heather started to say something first. I hope you don't mind."

Malory didn't answer. For a moment, Brittany thought she was going to blow up, so she thought *Spence Lake!* at her as hard as she could. Malory glanced at her and gave a slight nod. "Of course I don't mind. I'd rather walk with Spence anyway. Are you up for a little exercise, Mr. Lake?"

Art and Spence exchanged glances, then both smiled. The football players closed their books and left them on the table when they stood. "So what's up?" Spence asked. "Is this a group walk? Or something else?"

Malory looked to Brittany, picked up her thought, and said, "Group. For now, at least. Is that okay with you boys?"

"Just fine," Art said. "Where are we going?"

Malory smiled. "Into the woods."

Sixteen

Eve Camlan had lost all track of time, and existence seemed to come and go. Almost always, she felt as if she were on the verge of sleep, though sometimes she walked through an old town, encountering other people. Most were ghosts and never spoke, but some were more. Some were like her. Especially Holly.

Holly Gayle was the one constant. Whether she dozed or walked, Holly was always with her, a comforting presence.

The last thing Eve remembered was walking along the old road, passing amber lights in old houses, passing silent people. Now they were in an old church. The transition was sudden. One moment, she had looked up and seen the beautiful glowing jewels of the stained-glass window above them; the next, they were in this little hidden room, looking at their own physical bodies, bodies that clung together, just as their spirits did. Eve knew she was dead, and had known it from the moment Holly had called her out of the room in the smokehouse. *How long ago?* She didn't know. Now, she stared at the corpses in fascination.

Those bodies are ours! Eve Camlan's silent words were easily heard by her spirit companion.

Yes. I need to show you something. Holly, as

plainly visible to Eve as she was to Holly despite the darkness and the water, drifted forward, gently touching her own physical form, pushing chestnut hair from her face. She did the same to Eve's mortal body.

Why are we like this? Unspoiled? The others are all just bones.

I am going to show you why. I am going to show you our salvation. Holly turned to Eve and lifted the ruffles covering the bodice of her white gown. The dress's waist was revealed and with it, a green sash. In the center was a small silver dagger, shaped like a sword, slipped through the material to hold it together like a belt buckle. A large green jewel set into the ornate haft glowed with its own inner light.

Eve gasped and reached out to touch it, but her fingers passed through it and through Holly. It, too, was a ghost.

This was given to the creature we call Malory Thomas by the Forest Knight himself. It weilds great power. I took it the night I died. Malory still searches for it.

Does she know you have it?

She only suspects. She doesn't know where it is, nor does she know about my body, or yours. The stone in the little sword is what gives me the power to walk on land, and the power to save you.

I'm the only one you could save?

Yes, and only because you let go of your life before she expected you to. That is why you are here, with me. You share the power with me now. The stone is filled with real magick.

Is the real stone there?

No. No more. I used the power to move it to a safer

place. It was difficult to manipulate matter, but I fi-nally learned how. It's exhausting. I will teach you, but it takes time.

Where is it?

They drifted through the closed door, back into the main part of the church. Holly pointed at the stained-glass window. *Up there. Hidden in plain sight.*

How will it help us?

It will free us. It will free the other spirits as well. How?

Someone will help us, if she can. Someone of the same blood as Malory Thomas.

Confused, Eve stared up at the stained glass. *A sister? A mother?*

No. A daughter. The time is coming. We must help her. Other daughters have failed. Holly watched Eve. *What are you thinking?*

Can we go up and see it? The stone?

No. If Malory or a Fata Morgana were to come along and spy us, they would know and they would take it back.

What do we do?

Tonight is special. Malory may try to banish me, but she cannot. Tonight is a night of power for her, but even more so for you and me.

They were out of the church, drifting toward the surface. *Tonight, we will walk on land and try to make contact.*

With Malory?

Perhaps. But someone else as well.

Who?

Her daughter.

Kendra . . . The name floated into Eve's mind. *My roommate.*

You went to her briefly the night you died. You tried to warn her. Do you remember?

You helped me. She saw me, I scared her. She's Malory's daughter?

No. There is another.

Above the water, the half-moon wavered. Then they broke through the surface and the moon became solid. Eve looked at Holly, perfectly clear in the dark night. She looked at her own hands and saw that they seemed real. Around them, as they moved onto the shore—it felt like walking, but it wasn't, not exactly, for she couldn't feel the earth under her feet— loomed the woods. Behind them, she saw the Applehead Cheerleading Camp. It did not seem to be lit by the moon, as she and Holly were, but she could see more details in the darkness than she ever had been able to with her physical eyes.

Come with me.

Holly guided her forward, into the woods. The leaves of the oaks and liquid-amber trees were night-colored but she could see individual needles on the firs, veins in the turning leaves of the deciduous trees.

Where are we going?

To the Knight's Chapel, first. Then we shall decide where next to travel.

Seventeen

"The Shining game," Merilynn said, sucking the last of her lemonade through her straw, "was sort of about ghosts."

"Good heavens," Kendra said. "Is this another Barbie game, like *Exorcist* Barbie, *Return of the Living Dead* Barbie, and *Alien* Barbie?"

"Yes."

Sam picked a crumb of crust from the platter and popped it in her mouth. "I don't think you can beat *Alien* Barbie, Merilynn. Shaving her head takes the cake."

"Actually, that was *Alien Three* Barbie, but I guess the games all sort of ran together. I really liked *Aliens* Barbie. Putting her in the Transformer toy was fun. Even you would have liked that, Sam."

"Maybe. So what's *The Shining* game?"

"I know," Kendra said. "Barbie is Wendy and Ken is Jack Torrance. Skipper was Danny."

Merilynn smiled happily. "Exactly. I cut Skipper's hair for that too, so she'd look like a boy."

"What did your father think of that?" Kendra picked up her cup and poured some crushed ice in her mouth.

"He didn't care. In fact, he thought it was nice that

I turned one of my Skippers into a boy. I made a little Hot Wheels cart for him and everything. Of course, it was more like a wagon, but you know, when you're a kid, every cardboard box looks like a cave or a castle."

"Or a fort," Sam said. "I loved to build forts."

"You would." Merilynn laughed. "Father wasn't too happy with *The Shining* game after I made a miniature bat for Wendy and an ax for Jack." She paused. "But he complimented me on how well I could whittle."

Kendra laughed. "So, did he catch you swearing again?"

"I'll bet you were doing my favorite scene, where Wendy interrupts Jack while he's staring at his type-writer and he goes off on that rant about how when he's at the keyboard, he's working, whether he's typ-ing or not." Sam sounded downright excited. "I love that scene because it's true."

"No, sorry. He didn't like Barbie and Ken beating each other up, but he talked to me, you know, to make sure I knew good people didn't do that stuff. He was okay once he knew I knew. It was the blood in the elevator part that made him forbid that game."

"Blood in the elevator?" Kendra asked.

"You don't want to know. Even I knew I was going too far." Merilynn craned her neck to look at Kendra's watch. "It's going on nine-thirty. We should probably go back."

Sam nodded and all three stood up. Merilynn went to refill her lemonade and Kendra's iced tea while Kendra dug up two ones and dropped them on the table; none of them were sure if this was a place where you left a tip. The two waited by the door for Sam, who was at the counter, talking up the pizza guy. Finally, she joined them and they walked outside.

"So, look what I've got," Sam said. She waved a coupon for a free large pizza in front of them.

Merilynn gave her the eye. "Some reporter you are, getting paid off."

"Hey, we're students. I'm poor, aren't you?"

"Pretty much," Merilynn said. "I'm just surprised you're on the take."

Sam's jaw dropped, then snapped shut again. "I'm giving them a good review because they're the only game in town, but they don't have to know that," she said defensively. "And they didn't give me the coupon *before* I said they'd get a thumbs-up. They gave it to me after. So, technically, I'm not on the take."

"Would you have told them if you were going to write up a stinker review?" Kendra asked.

"Probably." Sam started toward the car, keys out. "Well, maybe not. But I wouldn't lie and say it was good when it wasn't just to get a freebie."

"I was teasing," Merilynn soothed. "You're so easy to ruffle. *I'd* give it a good review to get a free pizza even if it sucked. Well, not too much sucking. I wouldn't do it for a free pizza if I didn't want another pizza."

"Well, I wouldn't compromise like that," Sam said. She pushed the remote on her key, unlocking her little five-year-old white Camry.

"We know you wouldn't," Kendra said, waiting while Merilynn climbed into the backseat. She sat down and closed the door.

"That's why we love you, Sam. You're honorable."

"Merilynn, don't yank my chain."

"I'm not," Merilynn said. "You're honorable. You really are. I admire you."

"So do I," Kendra said.

Sam started the car. It purred.

"How do you keep this car in such good shape?" Merilynn asked. "It runs like new and it's so clean."

"My parents gave it to me when I left for Greenbriar. It's my mother's old car. She hardly drove it."

"She doesn't like to drive?"

"She loves to drive. She always took my father's SUV, so he bought her one too. She thought this car was boring because it's automatic, not stick." She pulled out onto the quiet main street of the town of Greenbriar.

"It's just so clean."

"My parents kept it that way."

"But you've had it for months. Where's all the trash?"

"Are you serious, Merilynn?" Kendra asked, looking back at her.

"She's serious," said Sam. "I bunked with her. She doesn't know how to put anything away."

"That's a quirk you didn't tell me about when you moved in," Kendra said.

"I'll be good," Merilynn said.

Sam laughed. "Just don't look under her bed, in her drawers, or her closet."

"Okay, I won't look. Merilynn, just don't leave gum on the furniture or clothes on the floor, and I'm cool."

"What if I leave them on my bed?" Merilynn prodded.

"That's fine. I just don't want to walk on them, okay?"

"No problem. Sam, you were one anal-retentive bunkie."

"The odd couple?" Kendra asked.

"We would be if we tried to share a room," Merilynn said.

Sam groaned. "Perish the thought." She halted for a stop sign.

"This place is absolutely dead," Merilynn remarked. "Greenbriar goes to bed early."

"It sure does." Kendra looked out the window. "I don't see anything open."

"There's not much here to *be* open," Sam said, peering in the rearview mirror as she accelerated. "We've got an asshole on our tail."

Merilynn looked around. Something tall with its brights on was coming up on them. "It's a truck or something," she said. "Maybe a Jeep. I think I see a roll bar."

"The wrestlers?" Kendra asked.

"I wouldn't be surprised," Sam said.

The lights were blindingly close, but she ignored them, flipping the nighttime switch on the rearview mirror to kill the glare and slowing down to twenty-five miles an hour.

"Are you trying to get them to pass you?" Merilynn asked.

"The speed limit in town is twenty-five. The place makes half its money ticketing speeding students. They aren't going to bully me into speeding."

"But you were going faster before they came along," Merilynn said.

"That was my choice. I won't let them make a choice for me."

Merilynn saw her smirky smile reflected in the center mirror. "You love this, don't you?"

"Is that wrong?"

"What do you think, roomie? Is she wrong?"

"I don't think so. I'd probably wuss out and pull over to get rid of them."

"I think they're the wrestlers," Sam said. "If we pull over, they will too."

Merilynn squinted back. "I think you're right. Two guys. Big ones. Yeah, I'm sure it's them."

"They'll follow us all the way back to the campus." Kendra sounded worried. "Once we're there, what do we do?"

"Don't be intimidated," Sam said.

"They're huge, they've been drinking, and we razzed them," Merilynn pointed out. "I know you're tough, but unless you have a gun or pepper spray or something, I don't want to mess with them."

"Nonsense. All we have to do is be confident," Sam said. "They won't come near us."

"Merilynn's right. I don't want to take that chance. When we get to the school, let's just pull up in front of the campus cop building. Just until they go away."

"Don't worry—" Sam began. "Damn it."

The wrestlers were flashing their lights at them now.

"I have an idea," Kendra said. "Pull over, but make sure they can't get in front of us or too close behind us. When they get out and walk up to the car, we take off, and leave them in the dust."

"That'd work," Sam said.

"Do you like the idea, Merilynn?" asked Kendra.

Merilynn had closed her eyes. She was concentrating, trying to call up that inner spark Father had helped her uncover.

"Merilynn?"

"Keep going," she said. "Just drive like you are. Give me a minute."

"What are you going to do?" Sam asked. "Moon them?"

"Not exactly. Just drive and don't make any smart-ass remarks when I say something weird, all right?"

"Sure."

Merilynn could feel Sam, could sense her concentration on driving. She also knew Kendra's eyes were on her, fascinated. That was a cool feeling. *I hope this works!*

"Wrestler boys drive wrestler toys. Roll-bar truck, now make a noise!"

Behind them, the vehicle backfired.

Sam laughed heartily. "If I were gullible, I'd think you did that."

"Shh," Kendra said softly. "She's not done."

"Frank Steiner and Norton Simms, your tires pop, you drive on rims!"

Merilynn opened her eyes and turned just in time to hear the *pop!* of a tire blowing out. The truck tilted slightly. Then three more *pops* sounded in quick succession. The vehicle sank and slowed behind them.

"They're on rims," Kendra said, awe in her voice. "Can you hear it, Sam? The metal?"

"I can. Merilynn, you have a lot of explaining to do."

"You mean you don't think that was a coincidence, Sam?"

"That wouldn't be logical," Sam said, sounding grim. "Unless you had it all set up in advance, and I don't believe that for one instant."

"She knows I never plan anything in advance," Merilynn said, pleased as hell.

"Explain," Sam said as they entered the tall wrought-iron campus gates.

"As much as I hate to do it, I'm going to invoke Gamma sister secrecy," Merilynn said. "If I tell you, you can never tell another soul."

Sam snorted. "Nobody'd believe it anyway. I'd lose my credibility before I even start my career. Don't worry. I swear on my honor that I won't talk."

"That's better than swearing on Gamma," Merilynn said.

"Much better."

"I swear on my honor and on Gamma," Kendra said.

"Okay. But, Sam, there's one other thing you have to do if you want me to talk."

"Name it."

"Tell Kendra what you saw in the boat that night on the lake."

"I don't know what you're talking—"

"Swear it or I won't talk until after you do." Merilynn sat forward as they pulled into the parking lot nearest Gamma House. "She already knows what I saw."

Sam pulled into a slot and turned off the engine. "I swear, I swear."

"Okay, I'll tell you later." Merilynn opened her door.

"Later, when?" Sam asked.

"In a little while. Let's go in for a bathroom break. Then we'll meet outside and talk."

"You're worried about being overheard?" Sam asked.

"You bet."

"Good," she said as they crossed the lot. "Me too."

Eighteen

Malory wished she had brought along the dregs of the vodka as the four couples walked into the forest. They had crossed the road and were deep in the woods now.

Her arm through Spence Lake's, they led the way along the path leading to the old chapel. Brittany, behind them with Perry Seville, radiated caution and Malory understood why. Things could happen here, this night, things might be seen that couldn't be explained to the quartet of jocks.

On the other hand, what could go wrong? If anything happened that they didn't want the boys to recall, she and Brittany alone could easily fog their minds. Hell, she didn't even need Brittany for that.

"I wish we had a better flashlight," Art said, shaking the penlight he'd taken out of his pocket when Malory lured them into the forest. She could see the shaky light on the path before her.

"It's okay," she said. "I know the way by heart."

"Me too," chirped Brittany.

"You girls must come here a lot," Duane said, from his position at the rear with Michele.

Malory's laugh hinted at sex. Brittany's giggle did the same.

"We've been here a few times, haven't we, Brittany?"

"I could live in the woods," her familiar answered, quite truthfully. "I love them."

They continued down the dark path. Malory saw well in the dark, Brittany even better, but the men didn't seem to think that was strange. She moved closer to Spence. All the males were thinking about was sex.

Which was all she really wanted to think about too.

They walked on for another ten minutes. The path, well worn, was smooth and she silently wove a spell for speed around them and found it commingling with one that Brittany had made. Her familiar sensed the connection. They traded smiles, never breaking stride.

"We're almost there," Malory announced as the trees began to thin. Soon, they entered a grassy clearing lit by the brilliant half-moon. She heard gasps from the males. Michele and Heather had been here before in moonlight like this and though it was breathtaking, they remained silent.

"The Forest Knight's Chapel," Malory said after they had gathered together.

"Awesome," Art Caliburn said. "I've seen it in the daylight, but this is something else."

What a way with words. Let Heather have him. "You've never had a nighttime tryst here, Art?" she asked coyly.

"Uh, no, not really."

"What about you, Spence?"

"Just a few daytime ones," he said, putting his arm around her waist.

"Perry?" Brittany asked her jock. "What about you?"

"I hiked out with a few of the guys once and checked it out. No trysts."

"I've been here at night half a dozen times," Duane boasted.

It was a lie. Despite its reputation, no one but the Forest Knight or a Fata Morgana dared stay here after dark. They had woven glamours around it to protect the sacred ground upon which it stood. Upon which they all stood now. The glamours frightened humans away. Heather and Michele would even be uncomfortable here and in fact, Malory could sense Spence's lowering libido, so she grabbed Brittany's hand—they stood side by side—and whispered, "Unlock with me" to her. Silently they said the words in unison.

Sexual tension soared back into Spence's aura. Malory prodded them all with a web of desire, trapping them. Only Brittany knew what she'd done.

"What do you think of the chapel of the Forest Knight?" she asked.

"Far out," Spence said.

Another brilliant one. Oh, well, he'll be fun to mount.

"It's just an old church," Duane said.

"An old church on sacred ground," Malory said. "This land has always been sacred and there have been other altars here, and standing stones. Some of the stones are incorporated into this incarnation of worship. Come on, I'll show you."

They approached the old chapel. Made of stone and mortar and wood, it stood tall in the clearing, its steeple intact, the window glass and doors long gone. Stepping through the doorway, they saw a bed of green grass and all looked up. The roof was gone, and the moon shone directly overhead, granting so much light that even the humans could see the inviting green of the grass.

"Wow," said some oafish male.

Brittany took her aside. "Was it wise to bring them here?"

"I don't know," Malory said, still feeling drunk. "Was it?"

"You want to fuck here?"

"Yes."

Brittany nodded. "Be alert. I'll warn Michele and Heather. We may have to cast a glamour."

"We could let them see Holly Gayle, if she shows up," Malory murmured. "That might be fun."

Brittany studied her. "It might be. But I wasn't thinking about Holly. I was thinking about *him*."

"Tonight?"

"Why not? It is his home."

"He will approve and let us be, if he comes along."

"Don't be so sure. He's hungry. He's waiting for a sacrifice."

"He's always hungry. Sex fills him."

"Caution, Mistress. Caution. Don't let your mind be numbed." Brittany nodded toward Heather, who was wrapped in a kiss with Art Caliburn. "Her mind is numb. She won't be of much use if something happens."

Malory shrugged. "She took what I wanted."

"It's just a man, no different from the one you have waiting. We need her."

"True. Don't worry, little one. Nothing will happen. Go."

As Brittany returned to Perry, Malory felt a slight

chill. Brittany's advice was always good, but she often erred on the side of caution. "Spence?" she said, walking up to her tall, broad-shouldered man.

"What?"

"Let me have some of your beer."

He smiled and handed it over. She swallowed it in one long gulp, then tossed the bottle in a shadowy corner and took him by the hand, leading him to the softest, thickest patch of grass in the shell of the chapel.

Tilting her head up, she kissed him quickly once, then again, more slowly, letting her tongue work over his lips, teeth and gums. She sucked his tongue into her mouth and felt his entire body shudder with desire.

"Undress me," she whispered.

He obeyed.

Out of the corner of her eye, she saw the other couples undressing, kissing, caressing, and the sight filled her full of lust, cutting through the alcohol, sharp and clear.

Spence laid her on the ground gently and stood over her, undressing. His body was magnificent, brown and clean, with a hairless chest, broad and muscled, and biceps that bulged. Between his legs, his erection grew into a fine fat sausage, and she hungered for the taste of it, for the feel of it inside her body. It had been too long.

"Come here," she said, hoarse with need. She tilted her legs akimbo. "Kneel here and worship at my altar."

Nearby, that little bitch Brittany giggled. She'd heard the silly words. Malory glanced her way, saw her rolled into a naked yin-yang ball with Perry Seville. Brittany wasn't looking, just listening.

As Spence knelt and put his huge hands on her knees, pulling them farther apart, she saw Heather pleasuring Art Caliburn and felt lust and anger; she would have that one too. She would have all of them before the night was over.

Spence's warm hands caressed her legs, pushing gently. "You're beautiful," he said. "Beautiful."

Malory looked at Michele. Already, the oafish liar Duane was mating with her, she on all fours, he ramming from behind. Michele's eyes opened wide with each thrust. Malory felt a sharp tingle as she realized Duane was using the other entrance.

"Make love to me," she said to Spence.

"Let me taste you first."

She almost laughed, but cut it off before it could escape. "I need you inside me," she insisted, still watching Michele's face.

"There's no hurry. I love to taste—"

"All right." She clamped her legs around his head and pulled him down. "Taste."

He was good for a man with a normal tongue. She watched the other couples mate as he worked. He built into a frenzy after her first orgasm, and she laughed softly and released his head, realizing she'd nearly suffocated him.

"Now," she said. "Fill me up."

Slowly, deliciously, he pushed toward her, showing a control that was agonizing and delicious. Finally, he filled her, stretched her, hurting her in the best way possible with his size. He began to move.

A banshee scream rent the air.

Nineteen

Kendra walked out of Gamma House at twenty past ten, wearing a fleece-lined denim jacket over an olive sweater, jeans, and her old Reeboks. She'd chosen the worn black pair over the new white ones at the last minute for a silly reason—the white ones were bright, easy to see. Why this mattered was a mystery to her, but Granny always said to follow her instincts, so on went the dark pair.

She paused on the veranda, feeling as if she was being watched, then walked casually—*I hope!*—down the steps and along the walk. The reflecting pool looked dark and chill beneath its clusters of lily pads. A frog croaked, another answered from the other side of the pool. A reply, a splash, another, a froggy tryst. All as she strolled toward the end of the pool.

As she approached, she saw a feminine silhouette rise from the bricks and turn. *Sam.* "Hi," she said.

"You're late," Sam said.

"Give me a break. We said around quarter after ten. We didn't synchronize watches."

Sam grinned. "Touché."

"Speaking of late, where's Merilynn?"

"I don't know. I thought she'd come with you."

"She took off before I had my shoes on."

"Pssst," someone whispered. "The cock crows at midnight."

"Merilynn?" Kendra said softly. "What are you doing?"

"Giving you the password. I feel like we're playing *James Bond* Barbie."

"Show yourself," Sam murmured.

She appeared so suddenly that Kendra jumped. "How'd you do that?"

"Where were you?" Sam chimed in.

"Wow, you two are easy to impress. I was just over there." She pointed at a single oak tree on the lawn near the forest edge.

"Bull," Sam said. "You did something."

Merilynn looked like a pixie in the dim light from the street lamp twenty feet away. Her green eyes glinted. "I stood in the shadow of the tree, that's all."

"But how'd you get here so fast?"

"I didn't. Look how far the shadow extends. I was only ten feet from you when I spoke. Almost at the end of the shadow. I just stayed very still. You didn't notice me."

"No magic, huh?" Kendra asked, still a little flustered and wanting to hide it.

"More like spy tricks. Sam, I know you know those tricks. You knew them back at camp. Keeping to shadows, moving slowly."

"Keeping to shadows, sure. That's common sense. I couldn't pull off what you just did though."

"Sure you can. I'll teach you. Both of you. There's nothing to it. So, let's get out of sight."

"No one can hear us here," Sam said. "No one but you could sneak up on us either."

"I want to walk a little ways," Merilynn insisted.

Kendra exchanged glances with Sam. "Okay," Sam said. "Lead on."

Merilynn led them to the sidewalk. They followed it as the lawn grew narrower and narrower, until the house was visible against the woods as glowing windows, nothing more. When the grass was only a two-foot-wide strip separating the sidewalk from the edge of the forest, Merilynn slowed and glanced around. "Follow me," she said and turned off the walkway, heading right into the forest.

They followed her into the shadows of the trees, out of sight, and then Kendra said, "That's far enough, Merilynn. Even James Bond would think this was a safe spot to talk."

"I'll say." Sam looked heavenward, then at Merilynn. "I have a class at eight A.M. I still have some reading to do tonight. Let's get this over with."

"Kendra," Merilynn said amiably, "Sam. What's today?"

"A school night," Sam said.

"Seriously, we talked about it earlier. It's an important one."

The first thing that went through Kendra's mind was that Eve had been dead exactly three weeks, but it wasn't exact. She thought a moment; then it hit her. "Of course! It's the birthday of Applehead Lake."

"And the death of the town of Applehead," Merilynn added somberly.

"The town was already deserted," Sam said. "It was already *dead,* if you really need to use such a dramatic word. Deserted is more accurate."

"The burial of the town, then. The *real* death. Until it was covered with water, it was still alive. People could have moved back in. Samantha Penrose, you saw those lights. You saw—tell Kendra."

Samantha's face cycled through several emotions; then she took on a look of sternness. "You tell us how you did the tire trick first."

"Sam, don't be a twit. Kendra, I told you about the ghost lights and about seeing Holly Gayle under the water reaching up."

"Yes, you did."

Merilynn turned to Sam. "You don't have to describe it. Just verify it. Did you see the ghost lights?"

"I saw something that couldn't have been reflections—I think. They appeared to be lights and *seemed* to emanate from under the water."

"Did you see the stained-glass window?"

"The window is in the administration building."

"You know what I mean."

Sam hesitated, looking as though she wanted to strangle Merilynn. "I saw something that resembled a stained-glass window, yes. But I don't know what it really was."

"That's fine," Merilynn said. "Kendra knows all about ghosts. She doesn't think you're crazy, do you, Kendra?"

"Not at all," she said. Then smiled slightly. "I wouldn't dare!"

Sam's face softened. "You've seen anomalies yourself?"

"Yes."

"Do you have any opinion about what they are?"

"I didn't, but recently I've begun to form some. Only begun. I don't claim to know anything."

"Okay." Sam cleared her throat softly. "I saw something that appeared to be a female ghost. Probably just like Merilynn described."

"I didn't exaggerate at all," she assured her. "It was Holly Gayle."

"That's an assumption," Sam said.

Merilynn's eyes flashed in the darkness and Kendra saw Sam flinch slightly. That amazed her.

"Samantha, it was an apparition. It was Holly Gayle. She matched all the stories."

"The stories assume it was a former student named Holly Gayle. There's no proof."

Now it was Merilynn's turn to roll her eyes. She was good at it, drawing it out, making her point.

"Let's call what you saw Holly Gayle, just for clarity's sake," Kendra said, trying to make peace.

Both the other girls looked relieved. "Maybe it was a hallucination," Sam said.

"Don't start."

"It could have been a shared hallucination, Merilynn. Stranger things have happened."

"You know that alleged hallucination was drawing you overboard. If I hadn't stopped you, you'd be at the bottom of the lake right this minute."

"Bullshit. I know how to swim."

"You wouldn't have had a chance. She was going to pull you down."

"You don't know that."

"Please," Kendra interrupted. "Please don't argue. Whatever it was, you saw it."

"Do you want to see it?" Merilynn asked.

"Me? What are you saying?"

"Tonight is the anniversary. The town always lights up on the night of the anniversary."

"That's just folklore," Sam said.

"There's usually some truth in folklore," Kendra said, trying to sound light to Sam and serious to Merilynn.

"When the town is lit, the ghost of Holly Gayle walks too." Merilynn made a sourpuss face at Sam. "According to legend."

Kendra shivered, remembering Eve, even now trying to recall her words. But all she could remember was the image, the chill, and the smell of the lake. "It's late," she said finally.

"Tell us how you did your trick," Sam said. "Now. A bargain's a bargain."

Merilynn glanced around. "Magick. Magick with a *k.*"

Sam looked annoyed. "Magick with a *k.* That's just New Age Wicca hokum."

"You're wrong." Merilynn looked triumphant. "Look it up, Sam. Magic is sleight of hand, tricks of a stage magician. Illusions. *Magick* is the real thing. I can do a little of that."

"A Catholic priest raised you and you think you're a witch?" Sam looked to the sky again, as if praying for release.

"It's not Wicca, I'm not a witch." Merilynn paused. "Well, maybe by some people's definitions I am, but not by mine."

"What do you claim to be, then?"

"Sam, cool it. You're going to burst a vessel."

"Let's hear her out," Kendra said. "Go on, Merilynn. What do you consider yourself to be?"

She shrugged. "Nothing. A little talented in ways we normally don't recognize. Maybe some senses science hasn't decided exist yet are more developed in me."

"What does your father think of it?" Kendra asked.

"He helped me understand it."

"I would think he'd want to have you burned at the stake."

"What's your problem, Samanatha?" Merilynn said sharply. "You should be half as open-minded as Father is."

"He's into religious dogma. How could I possibly be less open-minded than a priest? Less superstitious, yes."

"He's a theologian. If the diocese knew how open to everything he is, they'd kick him out."

"Why does he stay in the priesthood? Isn't that a lapse of faith, being open-minded?"

"Sam," Kendra said.

"It's okay," Merilynn snipped. "She's always been this way. She's got her ideas and she's sticking to them."

"Sorry," Sam managed. "This is all just so, so . . . illogical."

"Sometimes life is like that," Merilynn said gently. "Hey, don't give up your bite, Sam."

"I'm not." Her voice was ferocious.

"Oh, okay. Good. So, you want to see something?"

"Sure," Kendra said quickly. "Some magick with a *k?*"

Merilynn nodded, then eyed Sam. "If you look at me like I'm a bug under a microscope, it's going to be really hard for me to do."

"Sorry. Go ahead."

"Okay." Merilynn shut her eyes. "Be really quiet for a minute while I get it together."

They waited. The sounds of the forest, the crickets, the birds, even the wind gently soughing through

the trees seemed to grow softer and softer until silence surrounded them.

"Within this forest live many deer. Send me three,
send them near.

"Sorry, that was lame. I'm a little nervous," she
said, looking sheepish.

"No," Kendra whispered, feeling as if she might
float away. "Look to the right. But just move your
eyes."

They looked. Three deer, two does and a spotted
fawn, stood under an oak, waiting, sniffing the air,
calm.

"Shit!" Sam muttered.

Merilynn turned slowly, then walked to the animals, moving slowly and smoothly, holding out the
palms of her hands, murmuring. The deer stayed
where they were and let her pet them.

Sam took a step forward. The spell was broken, the
deer startled and fled.

Merilynn turned and smiled. Her eyes gleamed
green. "You can search me, Sam. I'm not carrying a
deer whistle."

"I don't think there is such a thing," she replied,
studying the red-haired girl. "Your eyes," she said finally. "Sometimes they're like the ones we saw on the
island. The reflections," she added, in a voice that
sounded forced.

Merilynn nodded.

"Is that part of why you can do these tricks?"

"Magicks," Kendra said quietly.

Merilynn cast a serene smile her way, then answered, "I don't know. I really don't. Maybe. But
probably not. Sometimes Father's eyes do the glowy
thing too."

"Really? They're the same color as yours?"

"Not so intense. I've only seen him do the glowy thing a couple of times. Me, I can't help it."

"You have your father's eyes," Kendra said.

"Only he's my uncle." She paused. "Though I'm not sure about that. I think he could be my father."

"Uncle is close enough," Sam said quickly. "Do something else."

"Three times the charm?"

"Yeah."

At that moment a scream tore through the forest, inhuman and horrible. Kendra saw Merilynn and Sam look at one another and knew they'd heard it before.

Twenty

Gliding through the woods, Eve tried to avoid trees out of old habit, but sometimes moved through them as she followed Holly Gayle toward the Forest Knight's Chapel. She felt alive, but not alive, awake, but also in a dream. She could neither smell the air nor feel it against her face in the ways she had while in her body, but now she was just as aware of it. Perhaps more aware of it than she ever had been. She *knew* the smell and feel, *knew* the taste. It was all so clear that it felt like her normal senses, just as her vision seemed to come through her eyes. But while she knew all of these things, nothing touched her, not the ground, not the trees she floated through. It was all separate, another world.

It is another world, Holly told her, reading her thoughts as if they were her own. *We are parallel to it. We live now in the land of spirit and you will see the magical beings you only heard of in fairy tales in your lifetime.*

Are they good? Are they evil?

Nothing is wholly good or evil. Things have leanings, tendencies, Eve. You have a tendency toward good. Malory has a tendency toward evil. But there are no absolutes.

Eve took in her surroundings, basking in her altered senses. *Are there fairies here? Trolls?*

She heard Holly's gentle laughter. *Yes. Though they are known by many names, in this forest you will sometimes see earth elementals called Puckwudgies. They are the servants of the Forest Knight. In the lake, you will see water elementals. Their special name is lost in this land, so the living call them undines, from the Greek myths. They are the same. There are elementals of air and fire as well. But none are so plentiful as the Forest Knight's minions.*

Eve felt delight. *Are Puckwudgies good or evil? I mean, which way do they lean?*

More tinkling laughter, like water in a brook. *They are neither, though their tendency is to be like their king, the Forest Knight.*

What is he like?

Eve sensed humans nearby, felt their life force. And a special place nearby.

A special place, Holly agreed. *The land sacred to the Forest Knight. He is the king in this realm, in this place. There are other kings in other forests, in deserts, in fields, in valleys and seas. Others like him and unlike him, but all are kings. The knight is made of all things green. A desert king is made of sand and blows like a whirlwind.*

Eve felt disquiet, in herself and from Holly. *What's wrong? Something's wrong!*

They defile the sacred land. And the Forest Knight knows.

What is his nature? Vague fear, leavened with excitement, filled her.

In reply, Holly filled her with pictures of trees and bushes, flowers and ferns. Butterflies, bees, a bird feeding its young in a tree. An odd little manlike creature with big eyes and green-gray skin moving among the shadows on the forest floor. And then glowing green eyes in a leafy face.

No! It killed me.

The knight did not kill you. Think, remember. Is the face I'm showing you so hateful as the one you saw? Are the eyes those of devils and demons?

Eve looked inside herself, and saw the picture Holly sent for what it was. A powerful face, frightening in its strength, but the glow of the eyes were not like the demon-slits that had visited her. No fat green tongue lolled. Leaves ran from each side of the knight's mouth, trailing into a beard lushly green and alive. There was humor in the eyes, if fleeting. *Malory killed me. She is like him?*

No. He is far more powerful, a god, the trickster god, and she is partly of his world, partly of the mortal one. She impersonated him to frighten you. She is not an elemental, but born human, long ago. She is like a Greek half-god. She buys immortality from the Forest Knight.

Then he is mostly evil? Eve thought of the sacrifices, of the bones in the submerged town, the spirits and ghosts that roamed its streets.

No. He is not evil or good. He simply is. *He is what others expect. He began with the first green sprout and will last until the end of this place. Perhaps longer. I don't know much except that he is far beyond much concern about the affairs of humans.*

Eve tried to understand, but everything Holly told her seemed to be at odds. *Malory gives him human lives. How can something that takes life not be evil?*

Holly laughed gently. *All gods take lives.*

Eve heard voices, saw the chapel, stark in the moonlit clearing. *Malory is in there. So is Brittany— Holly, what is she?* Though she couldn't see her, she sensed something unsettling about her, something wrong.

She is of the spirit realm, but able to take material form. Brittany is Malory's familiar and has been for many, many years.

She's bad.

She is what she is. She is a being who craves a master or mistress who is powerful in the ways of sorcery. She is Malory's creature. A long pause. Tension grew, thickening the air like cold syrup. The crickets and birds silenced. *Without her gemstone, Malory is less powerful than she could be, and without her familiar, her power further decreases. These are things her daughter should know.*

Who is her daughter?

You will see later.

Preternatural silence took the forest, but for the sounds of lovemaking within the chapel ruins. Abruptly, an unearthly shriek tore through the woods. It came from Applehead Island, and she remembered it from the day she, Merilynn, and Samantha had rowed to the islet and peered into the black cave. She had seen the eyes, then heard the screams.

It is the knight, Holly affirmed. *He is coming.* The spirit swirled around Eve, and swept her away, into the trees, out of the line of fire.

Another horrible scream tortured the air. Closer. *We should leave.*

There's no need. The knight will not harm us. He holds the spirit sacred. We are of his world. Holly pointed at the chapel as another cry sounded, closer still. *There are some in his chapel he will not deal with so kindly.*

Wind rose, howling, mixing with the screech, becoming one as they tore into the trees, spraying leaves and pine needles, furrowing the ground. In the center of the wind glowed the green orbs Eve remembered so well.

Ride the wind, Holly told her. She had joined with her, and that made Eve less afraid as they buffeted painlessly through the trees. They caught on the knight's wind and Eve thought they would be pulled along, into the chapel. *I don't want to go in there, Holly! I don't want to see!*

Don't worry. Holly surged around her, carrying her high into the sky, above the trees, above the wind.

Eve saw two figures run from the chapel, and come together and vanish. *Magick!*

Yes.

And then the Forest Knight exploded into his chapel, a tornado of screaming rage.

Human voices began to shriek in counterpoint.

Twenty-one

"Malory!"

Deeply involved in the depths that Spence Lake's varsity eight-incher could reach, Malory vaguely heard her familiar's voice call her name. She nearly answered, but the running back redoubled his drilling efforts and she gasped his name instead.

"Malory!"

Brittany, as delightfully naked as she could be, but stepping into her jeans, stood over them, looking urgently down into Malory's face. Spence made to pause and look up, but she forced his head back down and trapped his ass with her legs, scissoring up and down to make him keep moving.

What? She mouthed the word silently to keep the jock focused on his work.

"You heard him."

"The knight?"

"What?" said Spence.

"Nothing. Don't stop," Malory told him.

He grunted assent.

"I heard him." Brittany pulled her baby tee over her head, flipped it down to cover her breasts. "They heard him." She tilted her head toward the other couples. "They're getting dressed."

"Even Michele?"

"Yeah." Despite her concerned expression, Brittany smirked. "Duane's a quick-draw."

"His kind always are."

"Wha—?"

"Shh, Spence, just pump. Don't stop until I tell you to."

"'Kay." He started nibbling her neck.

"Mmmm. Brittany, I heard it. We've heard it plenty of times. It came from the island lair."

A new banshee shriek resounded through the air, slightly closer.

"He's coming."

"Yeah, yeah," Spence Lake grunted. And he did.

Malory let him finish, then pushed him off of herself. "Damn it, Brittany. I was about to climax."

"You idiot!" the little blonde sputtered. "I'm never going to let you drink again. You're going to get us killed! Now! Get dressed!" She bent and grabbed Malory's jeans and threw them at her.

Malory's sex- and vodka-soaked brain started to register the alarm in Brittany's voice. Still on the ground, she shook the pants, rolled back, and shoved her legs into them, then moved forward and up, pulling them over her ass. Brittany handed her her Gamma green T-shirt just as another shriek sounded, much closer than the last one.

"What the hell?" Spence said.

"Grab your pants and get out of here!" Malory ordered. The other three jocks stared at her, all of them pantless. "All of you! Out! Michele! Heather! It's him. He's coming."

"Who's coming?" Art Caliburn asked.

"The Greenbriar Ghost," Brittany said. "You guys get out of here."

"We're not leaving you girls alone!" Art yelled as the wind began to howl.

"No way," Spence said.

"You have to come with us!" Perry Seville said as he finished pulling his pants on. He reached for a shoe.

"Leave the shoes. Get out of here!" Brittany yelled as another furious screech rent the wind.

"It's a tornado," Art called. "We need to find cover!" He grabbed Heather's arm and pulled her toward the empty doorway, not bothering to grab her pants.

Brittany started to protest.

"Let him take her. She's too wasted to save herself," Malory told her. She raised her voice. "Get her out of here, Art. Now! We're right behind you!" Art nodded and picked the cheerleader up as if she weighed nothing and put her over his shoulder, fireman style. They disappeared into the night.

Wind tore needles from nearby trees; they struck Malory's face like hail. "Michele! Come on!" she screamed. "We need you."

Duane put his arm around Michele. The two other jocks just stood there like idiots and stared at the storm of leaves. Malory knew the humans, even Michele, were strongly affected by the sound of the Forest Knight's rage. It was the stuff of legends. "Get out of here!" she ordered, putting a boost of magick in the words to make them obey.

Art and Perry hesitated, looking dazed as the magick took; then they started running. Duane Hieman still held on to Michele. He didn't move, but stared at the sky.

"Look!" Brittany said. She pointed at the sky.

Beyond the swirling leaves, Malory saw the unmistakable flowing dress of Holly Gayle as the spirit rose above the wind. But it wasn't just Gayle. She surrounded another spirit. Malory squinted, saw pink clothing and blond hair.

"Damn it, Malory. It's both of them!"

Malory grabbed Brittany's hand and yanked her out of the chapel, into the clearing.

"What about Michele?" Brittany yelled in her ear as they embraced.

"No time. Do it. Now!"

They spoke the words that would move them to another place just as the Forest Knight's eyes became visible. They saw Malory and Brittany for a split second before the spell took and they left the place. As the chapel vanished, she saw the Forest Knight engulf it.

Twenty-two

Merilynn stood still, listening to the shrieks from childhood grow louder. Part of her wanted to turn tail and run away, back to the safety of the house, as Kendra and Sam were urging, but another part of her wanted to run forward to meet the power behind the voice, to gaze into those eyes she had seen in the cave so many years ago.

Not just the cave. Sitting in the boat, facing Applehead Island that stormy afternoon as Sam and Eve frantically rowed toward camp, she had seen him— the Green Ghost. *The Forest Knight.* She knew it absolutely now, as she listened, ignoring Kendra and Sam, shaking them off when they took her arms, so she could listen to the shrieks.

In the boat, she had seen the glowing eyes watching from the shoreline and had been surprised that they didn't follow them across the water; she knew that the ghost could do such things if it wanted. That day, through the rain, she saw the eyes and thought she saw the tall greenish form that owned them. The light was bad, the rain a torrent, so she had decided it was her imagination. Now she knew it wasn't. If she followed the sounds, she would meet the Forest Knight.

"He's going to the chapel," she said.

"What?" Sam said. The wind was gusting, blowing their voices away before they could be heard.

"It's the Greenbriar Ghost," Merilynn said, remembering that was how Kendra had identified the phantasm. *The elemental. Pan. Puck.* "He's at the chapel."

"Good," Sam said nervously. "Let's get back to the house."

Merilynn turned to look at the others. "The chapel isn't far. Wouldn't you like to see it?"

"No," Sam said.

"Where's your reporter's instinct?"

"Gone with the wind, Merilynn. That's a storm and it's headed this way. It could be a freak tornado."

"We're safe," she said. "It won't come here, across the road. The Green Ghost stays in the forest."

"We're *in* the forest," Kendra said. "Sam's right. It's not safe to stay here."

"He won't cross the road. It's too close to civilization."

"I don't think storms care about roads," Sam said.

"You can't claim you don't recognize the sound. I know you do."

"The island," Sam replied. "Of course I recognize it. There was a storm then too."

"The eyes—"

"Screw the eyes, Merilynn."

"You saw them."

"I did, but that doesn't mean they had anything to do with that shrieking wind."

"It's not just the wind and you know it." Merilynn stood straighter and turned to Kendra. "Do you want to see the stuff folklore is made of?"

Kendra's eyes betrayed fear, but there was tempta-tion too. Finally, she shook her head. "No."

"But you would have gone there before the shrieks. That's where we were going."

"I never agreed to walk all the way to the chapel tonight; did you, Kendra?" Sam asked.

"No," Kendra said apologetically. "I thought you might be leading us there, but I wouldn't have crossed the road."

"Me either," Sam said. "It's a school night."

The shrieks reached fever pitch and then there were more sounds, screams, human ones, very faint and small.

"We are *out* of here!" Kendra took Merilynn's arm and turned her as the screams faded.

Sam took her other arm as silence replaced the shrieks of wind and the Forest Knight. "Let's get back."

"Okay." Merilynn began walking with them. Deep and thick, the quiet felt like a quilt around her body, her ears, muffling everything. It wasn't until they reached Gamma House that the crickets and frogs began to make their night music once again.

They paused on the steps of the mansion and looked back the way they had come. "It's real," Merilynn said. "It's out there."

Twenty-three

The knight is gone, Holly told Eve when the wind died down. They still hovered above the trees. *Let's go down.*

Are you sure it's safe? Eve resisted Holly's attempt to move into a position over the clearing.

Even if he was still here, we would be safe. You must forget your fears. Come.

Eve let herself be guided over the clearing. Below, she saw bodies in the ruins of the chapel. She and Holly began to descend.

Not so fast.

All right. Slower then.

Eve looked over the entire clearing as they came down just outside the chapel walls. *Where did they go? Malory and Brittany?*

It is a magick they use. It's draining. No matter what we do tonight, they won't be able to stop us now.

They moved along the ground, just above it. Eve moved her legs—*phantom legs*—but knew she didn't really need to. Holly didn't.

If you ever want to scare the living, the girl told Eve, reading her thoughts, *don't walk. Just glide a few inches above the ground. It causes grown athletes to urinate on themselves.* She smiled at Eve. *It's re-*

ally quite amusing. Now come, let's go in. Don't be afraid.

All right. Eve was afraid anyway, but she tried to push the fear deep down where Holly wouldn't be so aware of it.

They entered the chapel from a small door space on the side. *Old habits die hard,* Holly said softly. *I still forget to just go through the walls more often than not.*

Two bodies lay in a dark crimson heap near the wider main entry. They seemed puddled in reddish shadow, but Eve knew what the shadow really was— their blood, soaking into the ground. She hesitated.

You may stay here, Holly told her. *I want to see who they are.*

Eve lingered behind as Holly glided to the bodies. She hovered around them, moving to look at them from different angles. Finally, she told Eve, *They are male and female. I think one is a Gamma, but I'm not sure. I don't recognize the boy. Do you think you could look?*

Eve didn't want to but . . . *I'm dead. It can't hurt me to look at death.* Haltingly, she walked forward.

It's an ugly sight, Holly warned, too late. *They've been flayed.*

Flayed?

Their skin is gone, except on the faces. The knight wanted them to be recognized. It's all right. Look.

Looking at blood makes me vomit. Or faint.

It will do neither now. Don't worry.

Eve covered the final few feet and made herself look. *Michele. That's Michele. One of the officers of Gamma.*

Then she is Fata Morgana too. She probably

*wouldn't have been here with Malory if she wasn't.
Do you know the boy?*

Eve forced herself to ignore the glistening pink
and red meat, the spill of intestines, and just look at
the face. *Yes. He's a football player for the Knights.
Duane, I think.*

Holly moved closer to Eve and urged her around
the bodies and out the main entrance. They saw no
one else for a few minutes, then suddenly encountered another pair, male and female. They were in a
small depression surrounded by ferns, still hiding.
The man wore only pants and was tending to the un-
conscious girl, who wore only a green Gamma shirt.

Art Caliburn, she told Holly. *I went on a date with
him. He's very nice. The Gamma is the captain of the
cheerleading squad—*

*Heather. She's the most senior human Fata Mor-
gana member right now. Come.*

Holly led her quickly through the woods. They
crossed the road and traveled through more forest, finally coming to the smokehouse where Eve had died.
They crossed the lawn, moving toward the house.

We're going in?

Absolutely. We have messages to leave.

Behind them, noises. They turned and saw Malory
and Brittany emerge from the woods.

Should we hide?

*No. They can't make us leave. Malory can't. Brittany
will try. Defy her will.*

Twenty-four

"Where are we?" Malory asked Brittany as the world returned. The forest still surrounded them, but it was a place she didn't recognize.

Brittany stepped away from her mistress, looking around before saying, "We should have agreed on a place in advance. Where did you will us?"

"I didn't think about it. Just a secluded place near the mansion. What about you?"

"I tried for your rooms upstairs. Obviously, it didn't work."

"I should have done the same." Malory was exhausted; the transport magick drained her energy. *If I had my stone, it would be nothing.*

"I have a feeling we're close to the house," Brittany said.

Wearily, Malory sank to the ground and put her back against an oak trunk. "I hope so. Do me a favor and scout?"

"Sure," Brittany chirped. She showed virtually no tiredness from their spell. Malory resented her ability to bounce back.

Brittany smiled, picking up Malory's thoughts. "You can't help being tired, Mistress. After all, you're part human. I don't have that problem."

Malory nodded. "I know. Go find out where we are!"

Nodding, Brittany moved away, trotting, sniffing the air, following her nose. Malory watched until the familiar whirled and shifted her shape.

A small striped chipmunk looked her way, chittering, then turned and raced off.

Malory waited, wondering what happened to the others, if they were still alive. She hoped so; she couldn't afford to lose two Fata Morgana members. She closed her eyes.

A few minutes later, she came out of a doze, feeling familiar little feet running up her arm. Groggy, she opened her eyes and stared into those of a chipmunk. "Get off of me," she said, exhausted.

The little bright-eyed creature hopped off, whirled, and became Brittany again. She held her hand out to her mistress. "We're very close. I think you brought us here."

Malory took her hand and sighed as she let herself be pulled to her feet. Hand in hand, Brittany led her through the dark woods.

"The animals and insects are back to normal," Brittany said. "It's over."

"I wonder if we lost anyone. I hope not. I hate messes."

"I'll go look after we get back, if you want."

"No, the knight is furious. I don't want you returning to the chapel alone, even in your other form. Tomorrow, after daybreak, we'll go survey the damage."

"We're going to need to do something about the jocks' memory."

"If any are alive."

"Look." Brittany squeezed her hand. "Can you see the lights?"

Relief swept over Malory as she spied upstairs lights coming from the back of Gamma House. They quickened their pace and came upon the smokehouse thirty seconds later. They walked around it, and came face-to-face with Holly Gayle and Eve Camlan, standing together on the back lawn.

"Damn it," Malory muttered. "I hate ghosts."

"Let's try to banish them."

"I'm out of juice, little one." They continued walking, arriving in front of the spirits, who glared at them.

"Get out of the way," Brittany ordered. Despite her chirpy voice, the command held power. The apparitions wavered slightly, but didn't leave.

Twenty-five

Merilynn and Kendra lay in their beds and talked softly of the Forest Knight, Eve, and Holly, for twenty minutes, both of them growing more alert despite the lack of ghostly visitors and the late hour.

Finally, Merilynn sat up and switched on her bedside lamp. "It's useless. I can't fall asleep when I know the ghosts are walking."

Kendra stretched and got up, crossed to the little refrigerator. "Want a bottle of water?"

"Let's make hot chocolate," Merilynn said as she walked over to the window and pulled the curtains back.

"Go down to the kitchen at this hour?" Kendra turned, hands on hips. "You just want an excuse to wander around and look for ghosts."

Merilynn laughed softly. "No, but I like the idea." She left the window and went to her closet, pulled a tall square duffle out. "I didn't unpack this yet," she said, putting it on her bed and unzipping it. "If I had, you wouldn't be accusing me of such things." She lifted a mini-microwave from the bag and put it on the dresser. "Plug this in someplace. I've got mugs and tons of packets of Swiss Miss."

"I'd tell you it was too late to be doing this," Kendra said, working, "but it sounds *so* good."

Merilynn placed the mugs—dark blue with gold stars glazed on and in them—on the dresser and Kendra poured bottled water into them then put both in the little oven and tapped it to life. "Four minutes?"

"Probably. It's not the world's speediest."

"You sure have lots of interesting kits. Herbs and stones, and mysterious powders . . . Like chocolate."

"I have my uses," Merilynn said as they returned to the window.

Below, the lawn and gardens were empty, lit by moonlight. "Mind if I crack the window?" Kendra asked.

"I'd love it."

Kendra smiled. "Eve hated the window open, but I like it cracked unless it's really cold out. I thought I was weird."

"If you are, so am I."

The window twist-lock was stuck but just as Kendra was about to give up, Merilynn produced a hammer-shaped silver tool from her herb chest. "It's to tenderize meat," she explained, covering the lock with a towel to dull the noise when she started rapping on it.

"I know what a meat tenderizer is," Kendra said as she went to add the chocolate to the hot water. "What I want to know is why you're carrying one. That's definitely unusual, you have to admit."

"Got it!" Merilynn announced. She opened the window wide. A chill breeze whooshed in as if it had been awaiting admittance. "Cripes, that's cold!" She pushed the glass down until only half an inch of air could seep in, then sat down on the bed and accepted the cup of chocolate from Kendra.

Kendra sat down next to her, cupping the ceramic mug in her hands. She hadn't expected the air to be so cold. "So, tell me about the meat hammer."

"People are tough." Merilynn's eyes twinkled like green Christmas lights. "You have to tenderize them before you eat them."

Kendra made a face.

"It's handy for crushing crystals and things. The pointy ends start the job, then I use the smooth sides to powder the crumbled material."

"Oh." Kendra blew on her chocolate. "I guess I liked the cannibal story better."

"I knew you would."

Twenty-six

"There, there, Mistress," Brittany soothed as she stroked Malory's forehead. "Everything will be fine."

Malory looked up into her familiar's bright eyes. "Your lap is nice and warm. Rub my temples."

Brittany obeyed. There was much she wanted to say to Malory, but none of it would make the sorceress happy and there was no point in talking to her while the dregs of alcohol still swam in her system. She moved her small fingers in smooth, firm circles over Malory's temples, then worked her way to the sinus cavities below her eyes, her touch always firm but never harsh.

"Ouch. No, don't stop. It's helping." Malory sighed. "Why did I do that tonight of all nights?" She stared hard at Brittany. "Why didn't you stop me?"

"Oh no, you're not going to blame me, Mistress. You chose to drink."

"I didn't remember that tonight was the anniversary."

"Really?"

Malory didn't answer for a long time. "Alcohol almost never hits me."

"I know that." Brittany moved her hands to the tight muscles in Malory's neck and began working them.

"And I would have stopped you if I had thought it would. It was a surprise."

"I don't like surprises," Malory told her. She sounded like a petulant little girl.

"I know you don't."

"I don't like that Merilynn moved rooms without asking permission."

"Brittany, you told Heather you didn't care at all. You acted like she was over-reacting by telling *you!*"

"Well, I didn't mind then. Now I mind."

"Why?"

"Too many surprises. Brittany, I've tried to figure it out, but I can't. What made the alcohol affect me so strongly?"

"I don't know, but I think magick could be involved."

"Who?" Malory came upright so fast that she bumped Brittany's chin.

"Ow! Lay down. Let me rub the tension away or you'll have a hangover."

"I don't get hangovers," Malory replied.

"You don't get drunk either." Brittany pushed her fingers lightly against Malory's forehead and the woman lay back down. "I don't know if anyone put a glamour on you. Probably not. It might just be an effect of the night. The anniversary. Holly's presence."

"That little dead bitch. I'll bet you're right. And now she's dragging Eve around with her. We have to put a stop to it before she gets stronger." She paused. "That's what's happening, isn't it, Britt? Holly Gayle's stronger than she used to be."

"Shhh. Calm down. You're exhausted. You must regain your strength. But yes, I think she's stronger."

"She raised Eve Camlan."

Brittany nodded. "She snatched her soul from us. And kept it with her."

"I'd kill them both a thousand times if they weren't already dead."

"We have to figure out why Holly is stronger."

Malory reached up and ran a finger along the side of her familiar's face. "We know why, don't you think?"

"Tell me."

"Because the Fata Morgana is missing a member? Two, now. Maybe three, if something's happened to Heather."

"Heather's fine. I checked while you were bathing. Art Caliburn brought her back to the house. He thinks they got lost in a windstorm and that Heather drank too much." She smiled. "Which is all true."

"He remembers nothing else?"

"No. I hope you don't mind, but I took it upon myself to cast a mild glamour over him and the other boys that survived. They'll all awaken with hangovers and no memories of being with us. Art won't even remember bringing Heather here."

"You're wonderful," Malory murmured.

"I know. But let's get back to Holly's power. I agree, it's growing. There's another reason."

"She has the amulet. I know it."

"Malory, stop trying to think until the alcohol wears off. We've always known she probably has it. Why else would she still be here, tormenting us?"

"Because she's a bitch."

"We've established that already, dearheart. Think another way. The Forest Knight was denied his sacrifice. He is angry."

"But we'll give him one on All Hallow's Eve."

Without thinking, Malory touched her own face, as if feeling for wrinkles.

"He won't deny you your immortality now, don't worry." Brittany leaned down to kiss her mistress's forehead. "He had the blood of one of our own tonight. He is sated for the moment. But we must complete the ritual of the thirty-first to truly please— and appease—him."

"I know. Tomorrow, we'll cover our losses and re-stock the Fata Morgana."

"Yes, that's a good start. But we must be wary about our choices. There is more to Merilynn than we know."

"You know what she is," Malory hissed. *"Who* she is."

"Of course I know. But the priest has influenced her. She may not be what you want."

"What? Do you know something that I don't?" Malory sat up again, took Brittany's shoulders and held them. "Tell me what you know."

"Mistress, I don't *know* anything. I have a *feeling.* That's all."

Malory ran her hands over Brittany's cheeks, her eyes bright and not entirely focused. "You make such a pretty little girl."

"Thank you."

"Do you really think my little Merilynn has been sullied by her father?"

"I don't know. We must be cautious. If we bring her into Fata Morgana without knowing everything about her, she could harm us."

"Perhaps we should simply pass her by for now. We can choose a couple of the lesser candidates and see what happens with her. We can test her." Malory laid her head against Brittany's shoulder.

"That's a good idea." Brittany stroked Malory's glossy dark hair, felt the warmth of her breath upon her breast. "I think she is powerful," she said softly. "I think she has inherited much from her mother . . . and her fathers." The last, she murmured. Her mistress had fallen asleep in her arms. Contented, Brittany gently lay back in the big bed and brought Malory with her. They tucked together.

Brittany listened to Malory's soft breathing but could not fall asleep herself. The night wind blew, the drapes billowed like ghosts. Brittany had cast a protection spell upon the house when they had come in, hoping it would be strong enough to deny entry to the ghosts. Now she shivered and silently cast another spell, one to keep their room safe from entry until Holly and her companion returned to the depths of Applehead Lake.

Twenty-seven

"Let's have a séance!" Merilynn announced as she wiped away a chocolate mustache.

"Girl, do you know what time it is?" Kendra was still wide awake and feeling very guilty about it.

"It's late."

"Past one."

"Want some more chocolate?" Merilynn took the empty cups to the dresser.

"No! I mean, I would, but I'll be peeing all night, so no!"

"Okay, you're right." Merilynn set the dirty cups and spoon in the refrigerator then unhooked the microwave and stowed it back in the duffle.

"Okay, why did you do that?"

"The chocolate won't be so hard to wash off."

Kendra nodded. That made sense, though the voice of her granny was having a fit about it inside her head. "Why put away the oven?"

"Are we allowed to have them?" Merilynn asked. "I read the rules, but you know, in one eye and out the other."

"I don't remember seeing anything about them in the rule book. I have the fridge, so I'm sure it's okay."

"Well, I'd rather put it away. Things get stolen around here."

"They do?" This was news to Kendra.

"Yeah. Little Lou, the cheerleader that was one of my old roomies, she had some underwear stolen."

Kendra snickered, feeling evil. "She probably lost it at a frat house."

Merilynn grinned. "Maybe, but she said it still had the sales tags on it. Red thong. Victoria's Secret."

"Thongs," Kendra said. "I tried thongs. Maybe it's just me, but I don't know how anyone can stand them."

Giggles spilled from Merilynn. "I know—and yuck! After a hard day irritating your ass, they must smell like an outhouse."

Kendra caught the giggles. "Maybe we're built wrong."

"Maybe. Do you wear high heels?"

"Not if I can help it," Kendra said. "I have two pairs for dressing up, but I hate them."

"Me too. I have *one* pair. Father got them for me for high school graduation. His idea. I thought I'd die."

"You and I are both abnormal," Kendra said with delight. "You know that, don't you?"

"I treasure it," Merilynn told her as she opened one of her bureau drawers and started digging.

"You're dropping your clothes on the floor."

"They won't go anywhere," she muttered. "Hang on. Got it." She pulled a flat wooden board out of the depths of the drawer. "Ouija." She set it down and bent, grabbing the fallen clothing and stuffing it back in the drawer. Then she opened another drawer and felt around, quickly pulling out a wooden planchette.

"Okay, let's have a séance." She brought the items over near the bed, stopping at her little yoga rug. She placed them on it and sat down cross-legged, looked at Kendra and patted the floor. "Come on."

Despite herself, Kendra moved to the floor. "I can't believe a priest would let you have one of these!"

"Father gave it to me. When they re-released *The Exorcist*, we got like a dozen of them. Parishoners turned them in. They were afraid." She paused. "That new scene of Regan doing the crabwalk on the stairs even scared me."

"Me too. But why did he give you this? I mean, aren't they considered evil by the Catholic church?"

Merilynn shrugged. "Probably. But Father's no ordinary father. Wait'll you meet him. He'd get kicked out of the church if the Popey guys knew what he does."

"Good God, Merilynn," Kendra gasped. "What does he do?" Visions of blood sacrifices danced through her head.

But Merilynn's eyes glinted green with merriment. She whispered, like the kid in *The Sixth Sense,* "He marries gay people."

Kendra stared.

"They generally frown on that. What did you think I was going to say? That he uses real blood for communion?"

"Something like that. That's nice, what he does. But wouldn't he get kicked out for the ouija board too?"

"I don't know. He keeps quiet. He likes his parish. The people. He likes helping them. It's a good job for him because it gives him plenty of time to study."

"He studies folklore?"

Merilynn nodded. "The occult, comparitive religion."

"Isn't that sacreligious or something?"

"Probably, but only if he went around preaching it. The church has nothing against scholars. That's what he is, a scholar. He doesn't talk about it to anybody but me."

"It? The occult?"

"Yes. Pretty much. He has an old friend that's like him, another priest who studies weird stuff. He talks to him sometimes. He's sort of a mentor. Father Tim gets assigned to a lot of traveling jobs though, so he's not around much." She looked down, pushing the planchette around with one finger. "I hope he's around now. Uncle Martin—Father—is probably lonely. He doesn't admit it in his e-mail, but I can tell."

"He sounds nice."

"Wait'll you meet him. You'll love him." She paused. "He has eyes like mine."

"Those are some powerful eyes, Merilynn. On a priest, well, he must be killer at Mass."

She twinkled. "He's not bad. Women are always trying to get him in the sack. Men too. He's a cutie."

"But he resists? Both?"

"He's straight, so guys are easy to resist. He tries not to be alone with women on the make. I don't think he's ever been seduced, but then none of us can stand thinking of our parents having sex, right?"

Laughing, Kendra nodded, then shivered as a trickle of cold wind entered the room. "So, let's do this. We have to get some sleep. At least I do."

"Okay, put your fingertips on the planchette. Very lightly." Merilynn did the same. "Now, we close our eyes and concentrate."

"On what?"

"On calling spirits to visit. I'll talk. You just concentrate."

"Okay." Kendra's spine prickled up with goose bumps, but she hid her nervousness.

"We call to any spirits who are listening," Merilynn murmured. "We call you in peace and kindness and love. We call you to come and talk with us." She was silent for several moments. "Spirits, you are welcome to join us . . ."

The temperature seemed to drop. *I'm just freaking a little.* Kendra ignored the sensation as best she could, but she opened her eyes. Low light filled the room, Merilynn sat before her, as serene as a madonna.

"Spotty," Merilynn said abruptly. She opened her eyes. "Spotty?"

Kendra couldn't speak.

"Does that mean something to you?" Merilynn asked. "I hear a voice saying 'Spotty.'"

"Oh my God, you couldn't know about that!" Kendra snatched her fingers off the unmoving planchette. It felt ice-cold.

"Wait. What? Tell me! Don't get up!" Merilynn grabbed her wrist, forcing her to stay.

"You couldn't know."

"I *don't* know. Tell me."

"It's a horrible old high school nickname," Kendra said. "I never told anyone but Eve, the day we moved in together. I'm sure she didn't repeat it. I had a little accident. Some cheerleaders nicknamed me 'Spotty.' I told her. You know," she added, trying to shake off her anxiety, "Eve and I were bonding."

"Evie wouldn't repeat that," Merilynn said. "She used it to show you she's here. To make sure you know it's her."

"I don't know. Malory and her Gamma girls could have dug that up when they were checking me out."

"And they told *me?*" Merilynn looked ready to get royally pissed off.

"No, no, of course not. I just mean, somebody could know."

"And what? Send me signals on some freaked-up radio wave?"

"No!"

Finally, the redhead smiled. "I'm giving you a hard time because you're looking for hard answers when there's a simple one you just don't want to accept. Eve is here. We saw her outside. We saw Holly Gayle."

"You're right." Kendra rubbed her arms. "I'm just spooked."

Merilynn studied her. "Spotty, huh?"

"For quite a while."

"Then the Gammas probably know. Some of them probably do."

"Heather," Kendra said. "Head cheerleader. She'd know."

"Want to have some fun?"

"I've had all the fun I can stand. I really don't want to talk to any ghosts tonight."

"No, no. I mean *fun.*"

"Sleep would be fun."

"Yes, but after some real *fun*. Some instant karma. I mean, don't cheerleaders—except you, Eve—" she added, looking up and around, still hoping for contact, "really irritate you?"

"Of course. That's their job."

"High and mighty. All cliquey."

"I'm with you."

Merilynn stood up and ditched the ouija board, much to Kendra's relief. She then opened her chest of herbal medicines, powders, oils, and heaven knew

what else, and selected a small pouch of fine reddish
power. She brought it and a piece of paper to the rug,
placed the paper on the rug and opened the plastic
pouch, took a pinch of the reddish powder.

"Concentrate," she said.

"On what?"

"On what I'm about to say."

Kendra nodded.

Merilynn began to slowly let the reddish grains fall
to the paper, speaking softly:

"I wearied of my period and sent it off to you

"Gamma cheerleaders wake up red, Aunt Flo's
come and stained your bed

"Tampon strings and pantiliners, maxipads without wings

"My spell binds you to all these things!"

Kendra couldn't help it; she started laughing.

"What?" Merilynn asked, her smile sly.

"That was mean."

"I told you, instant karma."

"You really did it?"

"I feel like it worked."

Kendra stifled another laugh; it came out a snort.

"It won't hurt them, will it?"

"Nah. They'll just be surprised. Same old, same
old, otherwise. Nothing Midol won't cure. But I did
curse their supplies. You noticed?"

"I didn't realize."

"Intent," Merilynn said. "Tampon strings will fail
and liner wings won't stick right. They're going to be
a little cranky."

Kendra was holding her stomach and rocking, trying to keep her laughter and voice down. "How will
we know if it worked?"

"Oh, I think we'll know when they come begging for Midol and tampons that work right." She hesitated. "But just to be sure—I mean, we're lowly freshmen, they probably wouldn't come to us—let's add something they can't hide. And maybe spread it out a little."

"You look like a little devil."

"Thank you. Now concentrate:

"Gamma senior sorority lasses, listen to me now:

"May your asses fill with gasses

"Noxious fumes and evil perfumes

"For twenty-four hours, your farts could kill a cow!"

Kendra held her breath, trying not to laugh. "Just seniors, right?"

"Right. I suggest we skip breakfast."

"You're mean."

"Nah," Merilynn said coyly. "Just a little wicked."

"Raised by a priest and you do this!" Kendra teased.

"Must be my mother's side coming out!"

"Was she evil?"

Merilynn shrugged. "I don't know anything about her. Father didn't know much, there were no grandparents, yada, yada, yada." She rolled her eyes. "I never knew her and she's dead, I guess. Unless she ran off and Father just played the gentleman." She fell silent.

"It's two in the morning," Kendra said, rising. "I have to get some sleep."

"Yeah."

Twenty-eight

Brittany awoke from a fitful doze to the sound of a long, thin whistle that faded away as she listened.

Malory still lay nestled in her arms, breathing softly, regularly, fast asleep. She studied her mistress. A beautiful sorceress, centuries old, milky skin, hair like ravens' wings, lush mouth, sooty eyelashes, arched eyebrows, perfect cheekbones, a nose any woman would want.

Lower, her long neck and shoulders were naked above the covers, the satiny sheets and forest green velvet spread. Perfect flesh but for slight goose bumps from the cold air swirling in from the window.

Brittany lifted the covers to pull them higher just as another long, high whistle filled the air. Gagging, she expelled her breath and clamped the covers down as her mistress's ass sang its dirty tune. Malory didn't move until Brittany tried to ease out of her arms.

"Don't go, my little love," Malory murmured, mostly asleep, oblivious as a fresh whistle rose.

"Bathroom," Brittany murmured, loathe to wake her mistress. "I'll be right back."

"No," Malory muttered in her petulant child tone. "Stay with me." Her grip tightened.

Trapped, Brittany endured, but she'd rather have slept with ghosts taunting her than the foul odors coming from her mistress.

Twenty-nine

"I guess the ghosts aren't going to visit us tonight," Kendra said, slipping between her sheets after a quick trip into the bathroom to be rid of excess chocolate milk. Bed never felt so good.

Merilynn, already in her bed, said, "I guess not."

She sounded so regretful that Kendra felt sorry for her. She also felt guilty about bringing up the girl's missing mother. Making amends, she said, "The idea frightens me, but I'd still like to see them. Eve and Holly."

"There's nothing to be afraid of. Holly and Eve would hate the Fata Morganas, not us. We're Eve's friends. Or at least you are—and I don't think she would come here to scare me, even if she's not too crazy about me." She yawned so hard her eyes watered. "She couldn't scare me anyway."

Kendra chuckled. "I don't think anything could scare you. You're more fearless than Sam. I couldn't believe you wanted to go to the chapel and try to see the knight!"

"Maybe I'm just crazy. I have to warn you—I lack common sense. Nobody's braver than Sam. I mean, how can you compete with that attitude? It's not just show either. You should have seen her back at camp. She's a rock."

"Maybe we could walk out to the chapel tomorrow," Kendra said softly, still feeling regretful. "My last class is at one. I could be ready at two-thirty. We could go then."

"I'd love to."

"It's a date." Kendra closed her eyes.

Thirty

Merilynn listened to Kendra's soft even breathing and felt herself start to drift off, began to see quick flashes of near-sleep dreams.

Then the air pressure changed. It pressed on her ears, so gently she barely felt it at first.

Steadily, it increased, then the hairs on her arms began to stand, the hair on her head to crackle against the pillow.

"Merilynn!" Kendra called out in the dark. "What's happening?"

"It's okay, Kendra," she said, not trying to hide her excitement. "It's just static electricity. Stay still. Leave the light off."

"Meri—"

"Shhhh. Don't be afraid. Keep your voice down."

She barely got the words out before the air in the room grew chill. "Holy crap," she murmured. "I think they're coming after all! To visit—"

Holly Gayle and Eve Camlan glided through the closed door as if it weren't there. The chill grew as they drew closer. The cold odor of the lake filled her nose.

Kendra.

Eve's voice. Merilynn glanced at Kendra. She was

staring at the phantom in the pink sweater and jeans. She could hear the voice too, this time.

Kendra. Eve's spirit gazed at her former roommate with fondness.

"Eve," Kendra choked out. "I saw you before."

Yes. I wanted to warn you. They drugged me. They were going to sacrifice me to the Forest Knight. But I died before they could. Holly rescued me.

"They?" Kendra asked.

The sorceress and her familiar. Holly's voice sounded clear and pure, like water, and her eyes locked on Merilynn's. *They are dangerous.*

Holly glided toward her, silently, smoothly. Merilynn felt a shiver of fear. "Kendra?" she whispered.

She didn't answer.

She sleeps now. Holly hovered over her. *This is for you to know: The living daughter of Malory Thomas can release us.* Holly's eyes were dark, hypnotic, like so long ago on the lake.

"Do you want me to find her for you?" Merilynn asked nervously. The ghost did not feel friendly.

You know of whom I speak.

"I don't."

In your heart, you know full well.

Merilynn's mind reeled. "Me?"

You. The sorceress consorted with the Forest Knight then appeared to your father in a dream and used his seed to complete your conception.

"My real father died."

No. Your true father is the priest. You know this in your heart as well. You are as Malory's teacher was: the product of a union between a man of the cloth and a magickal being of evil intent. Her teacher's father was a demon, her mother a nun.

"Does Father know he's my real father?"

Yes. He knows many things. He can help you. The image flickered slightly. *There is more to tell you but we are nearly out of time. There are those who would keep us out of this place. We must go.*

"What do you want me to do?" Merilynn begged.

In response, Holly lifted the ruffled bodice of her white dress to reveal the jewel set in a silver knife that glowed the color of the Forest Knight's eyes.

The color of my eyes sometimes, Malory thought.

Yes. Holly had heard her thought. *You have two fathers and the knight is one. Listen to me. You can release us and all those others trapped under the lake if you can find this dagger and kill your mother. It is the only way she can be killed.*

"Where is it?"

I will show you in your dreams. Holly and Eve floated backward toward the door. *Sleep now.*

Then they were gone.

Thirty-one

Morning sunlight woke Kendra. She stretched, enjoying the warmth of the covers, still drowsing. Until she remembered their visitors. She sat up instantly. "Merilynn!"

The girl didn't answer. Kendra jumped out of her bed and went to Merilynn's empty one. There was a note, just two sentences:

Kendra, I know where the knife with the stone is and I've gone to get it. Don't tell anyone.

Love, Merilynn

Please turn the page for an exciting sneak
peek of the next book in Tamara Thorne's
Sorority Trilogy

SAMANTHA

Coming next month from Pinnacle Books!

The Sorority
SAMANTHA

You're one of them . . . or you're dead.

At exclusive, isolated Greenbriar University, within the elite Gamma Eta Pi sorority, is a secret society known as the Fata Morgana. Its members are the most powerful women on campus—and the deadliest. For this is a sisterhood of evil, a centuries-old coven, and every girl who pledges herself to their wicked decadence does so for life . . . or death . . .

HOUSE OF HORRORS

Tough, tenacious Samantha Penrose knows there's something going on inside the secluded, creepy Gamma Eta Pi mansion—somthing that may be connected to Eve Camlan's "suicide" and Merilynn Morris's unexplained disappearance. And the ambitious journalism major is going to get the story, even if she has to make herself over as the ultimate sorority girl to do it. As a new pledge, Samantha takes every opportunity to explore the hidden, off-limits rooms of the old house, searching for links between other mysterious deaths on campus and the Fata Morgana. But the secrets she uncovers are more than scandalous . . . they're downright sinister. There's the disturbing way Malory seems to watch Samantha's every move . . . the strange chanting coming from the forbidden east wing . . . and the chilling, ghostly messages she can't ignore . . . desperate warnings to run— while she still can . . .

Applehead Lake
Cheerleading Camp
Eight Years Ago

One

Meteors showered the black velvet night. *The Perseids.* Samantha Penrose lay on her back just inside the treeline not far from the cabins and tried to concentrate on the annual mid-August display.

It wasn't easy. Tree limbs blocked much of the view, but the only other place nearby—*the best place*—to view the meteor shower would be from the shadows of the dock or boathouse. *That's where you should be. What are you, a coward?*

Maybe I'm just smart. She wiggled a little, trying to get more comfortable on the loamy bed of ancient oak leaves and pine needles. After what she and Merilynn had seen under the lake two nights ago, she really didn't want to approach the lake or its creaky old structures at night.

By herself.

You're chicken! taunted her inner bully.

No, I'm exercising caution! retorted her inner reporter.

Sam craned her neck as a bright flash fled across the sky and quickly disappeared behind the trees. She knew all about people who weren't cautious; they were the ones who got killed when rock-climbing because they didn't bother to check their ropes, or murdered because they pretended it was safe to walk down a street alone even though everyone knew muggers struck there. If you had to do something risky, you went prepared, alert, confident, but as her father always told her, you darned well better not do it just to show off.

Lurking around the dock and boathouse would have been showing off. Definitely. And just standing out there in plain sight on the beach would be even stupider. *You know you don't want to go near that lake anyway.*

If she had brought anyone with her, she might have been tempted to approach the water, and that was part of the reason she'd slipped out of her cabin at one in the morning all alone. Her father always said that taking stupid chances had to do with your inner bully wanting to get loose and show off—or other people's inner bullies daring you to. He said it was more of a man thing, usually, but that she was a chip off his block, not Mom's, so she should learn from his mistakes.

He'd made lots of them, he told her. He couldn't resist a dare when he was young and ended up breaking his arm twice and his leg once. The worst was the time he'd gone up the stairs of the local abandoned "haunted" house (three stories of peeling white clapboard) while the other boys watched—that was when he broke his leg. It wasn't because of imagined ghosts or guys trying to scare him, but because his foot broke through one of the stairs and he crashed through the rotted wood halfway up his thigh before his leg snapped.

He was full of stories like that. He finally learned his lesson in Vietnam. Despite broken bones, sprains, stitches, and a concussion at the age of ten when he took—and won—a bet that he couldn't make his swing go over its A-frame in a complete circle, he had still believed, at nineteen, that nothing could kill him. He did all sorts of stupid things. Bullets barely missed him as he took chances the others in his squad wouldn't. He loved the feeling it gave him. But finally, shrapnel got him. Even now, Sam wasn't sure what shrapnel looked like, or even what it was, but she pictured hunks of twisted knives. The surgeons had removed pieces from his abdomen—he had shiny scars that were pretty cool-looking—but they'd also had to remove his left hand and arm, halfway to his elbow.

That wasn't cool, not at all, and it was why she listened to him. His missing hand gave her nightmares when she was younger. Even now, sometimes. She shivered despite the warmth of the night. *Don't think about it!*

Thinking about things that scared you could get you in trouble, too. Old dreams about crawling hands climbing her bedspread, moving over her covers, dripping blood as the fingers moved steadily toward her neck, suddenly flashed through her head. The hand never looked like Thing in *The Addams Family.* The one in her dreams had a ragged, bloody stump, meaty, with white bone shards sticking out of it like needles.

Stop thinking about that! I have to be on alert. I can't let anyone catch me out here! Only two more days and this stupid camp is over. No more dumb cheers. But if they catch me, they'll make me practice extra time until it's time to go home! Yuck!

The horror that thought stirred was preferable to

the kind brought on by thoughts of severed hands. It buoyed her, and she concentrated on the sliver of sky visible between the trees. Soon, she felt no fear at all, just irritation at how little of the sky show she could see.

Quietly, she rose and brushed away the brown leaves sticking to her legs and shorts. Walking to the very edge of the forest, she stood in the shadows of the trees that met the lakefront beach—*don't move, people who move get caught*—and studied the sky. The still air, retaining dregs of daytime warmth, smelled pleasantly of pine and earth. The view here was much better, but it was easy to look at the lake too, and she really didn't want to look at it.

That's as silly as being afraid of a crawling hand.

She made herself look at the lake. It was a good twenty yards distant. It gleamed darkly, a black jewel, unfathomable. Far out, a low mist hung a foot or two above the water. Undoubtedly, it shrouded the island; she couldn't even see its silhouette. The moon hung coyly low, flirting with the tops of the trees, and what light it shed left Applehead Island completely untouched.

Calm now, in control, Samantha returned her gaze to the velvety clear night. Stars twinkled, planets glowed steadily. She picked out constellations: Leo, the Big Dipper. Smaller, more distant, her favorite, the Pleiades. *The Seven Sisters.* Mythical, magical, sisters. She liked mythology, especially Greek stories of gods and demigods.

The still warmth was broken abruptly by a stray breeze. It felt good against her face, holding a hint of coolness, no doubt from the lake, for it brought with it the faint dank cold-water smell. It gave her goose bumps, bringing the image of the ghost of Holly Gayle staring up at her from beneath the lake surface. *Stop it, right now! Maintain your control!*

The breeze continued, strengthened enough to ruffle her bangs, and she thought she heard faint voices come with it. *Singing?* It was too soft for her to be sure, but it made her think of times when the water pipes in her home vibrated just right. Her dad had explained how that worked, dispelling imagination with science, but it still reminded her of distant feminine voices singing, almost chanting. She thought that sound was what the Sirens of myth sounded like as they lured sailors to their deaths.

Now, in the woods, the voices grew clearer but remained too faint to be truly recognizable as human. Not birds, no, but probably the wind vibrating leaves the way water sometimes vibrated through the plumbing. She cocked her head, forgetting the sky, enchanted by the music.

It sounded closer as the breezes increased.

Five minutes passed before she decided that what she heard truly were voices. *Not too far away . . .* She was drawn to them. *I can walk along the edge of the forest. No one will see me.*

For an instant, she hesitated, wondering if she was being foolish, like the sailors who listened to the Sirens' call. *Maybe.* But as long as she stayed away from the lake and kept to the shadows and paid attention to where she stepped, why not? Reaching in her pocket to make sure the short packaged lightstick hadn't fallen out—*I probably won't need to break it open, but I have to be prepared!*—she began walking toward the singing.

Two

Skirting the lakefront, moving from tree to tree away from the cheerleading camp, toward the voices singing somewhere along the eastern side of the lake, Sam imagined she was a native scout, sneaking up on buffalo killers, then switched to pretending to be Jane Bond, girl spy. By the time she had turned to her favorite game—investigative reporter, about to break open a story—the singing was very clear, though she couldn't understand any words.

Forgetting the games, she paused to look back at the camp, seeing little but the sodium glow of a few tall lamps among the trees, a suggestion of a square building or two, and the hulk of the boathouse and short length of dock. She wasn't sure how far she'd come—*a quarter mile, an eighth?*—but the camp looked small and far away. It lay at the short south end of the oblong lake and she was well away from there now, definitely on the lower eastern side.

The Song of the Sirens. Listening to the a cappella voices, she felt a surge of fear, but it passed quickly. The choral music rose and fell, so beautiful, so foreign. The tone grew more intense, stronger paced, as she listened. It was building to some sort of climax

and the beauty and intrigue compelled her to move
on despite the danger. *Alleged danger.*

No longer playing pretend, not even thinking of it,
but relishing the adrenaline rushing through her, she
kept to the shadows, as close to the edge as possible.
It seemed darker here. *It is darker. You can't even see
the moon from here!* She patted her lightstick, safe
and sound in her pocket, but didn't even think of
using it yet, not as long as she could see by the dim
phosphorescent gleam of the pale beach sand.

The voices rose higher and stronger, flavored with
a tinge of ugliness in the foreign words that stained
the beauty of the choir. She moved forward ten more
feet and stopped. The music came from within the
forest—directly within.

There was a well-worn path to follow. She turned
onto it and faced the trees, thinking that this was the
end of the line. If she used the lightstick, someone
might see it, but how could she walk into the trees
in near blindness? *You can still see the path a little.
Just stay on it and go a little ways. Just until you
can't make it out anymore. It's what a smart reporter
would do.*

Reporters, her father had told her when she asked,
usually had much longer life spans than spies, and
agreed that journalism would probably be a more
rewarding career. When he'd said that, he was ban-
daging her magnificently skinned knee. Finished,
he told her, *You have to be cautious now so that you
can grow up and become what you want to be.*

The path was pale bare dirt, mixed with sand at
first, and as long as she walked very slowly, she
could make it out. The choral sounded closer, wilder
yet still oddly religious. *Just a little ways farther,*

she promised herself. *Stay in control, don't take risks.*

As she crept along, a slave to her curiosity, it suddenly occurred to her that these voices might not belong to students from the college or girls from camp, maybe some counselors. Sure, camps had sing-alongs, but this didn't sound like anything associated with roasting marshmallows.

Telling ghost stories, maybe.

She shivered and stumbled as the all-but-invisible path jogged. She paused, her eyes on the ground, her ears entranced, her nose full of earth and pine and lake smell. And fire. Just a hint. A campfire, a bonfire, but not a forest fire. Slowly, she became more aware of the trees pressing in on her, of the voices, singing so close—*it's the way the wind is blowing, they can't be that close!*—of the lack of other forest sounds. Nervously, she continued to look down, and could barely see the outline of her shoes, let alone the path. *This is it. Time to turn back.*

And then she looked up.

In the woods, not too distant, she spotted a small square of firelight—*the bonfire.* It was as if she were looking at it through a window, but that didn't make sense, nor did the color of it—the flames, if that's what they were, had a greenish tint.

Sam realized she was trembling. *You can change the color of fire with chemicals you toss on it.* Or maybe it was just the green of the trees casting strange reflections. The chorus lowered, then rose again, frenzied, reminding her of church music, weird church music. And then she realized she was looking at the old chapel.

The haunted chapel.

A few days ago, she would have laughed off the haunted part. Now she wasn't so sure. Voices rose impossibly high and, for the first time, they reminded her of the banshee howls on Applehead Island.

They don't sound anything like the howls did, her inner bully said.

No, but they still remind *me of it,* replied the wary investigator within.

She'd come so far that she decided to continue on. Soon the fiery greenish gleam coming from the window threw enough light to let her see the path. Silently, she moved forward and the size of the window grew quickly. She was nearly there. Singing filled the air. A few more steps and the trees ended, encircling a broad clearing as they did the lake. In the middle of the clearing stood the ruins of the chapel. *It's a make-out spot.* But it sure didn't sound like anyone was making out in there.

Swallowing, she crouched low and fast, covering the space to the window in twenty steps. She stayed slightly hunkered beneath it as she worked up her courage to look in. She took a deep breath, exhaled slowly, and studied what she could see of the building. There were actually two small windows: this one, which had been her beacon, at one side of the small chapel, and another, just like it, at the other side. The blank center of the stone building must have once been behind the preacher's pulpit.

Slowly, slowly, she rose, leg muscles tight and tense, and peered into the window.

The fire burned about ten feet away, casting eerie light and shadow on green-robed figures gathered beyond. They were hooded, covered from head to knee—which was as far down as Sam could see.

Standing in a circle, their arms were raised and hands were held. They continued to sing and Sam couldn't see what, if anything, was in the middle of the group. Rising higher, calf muscles trembling, threatening to knot, she saw their feet.

They were all floating a foot above the ground. *Nah, don't be ridiculous. Only half a foot.*

Sam nearly laughed, forced herself to maintain control. *No! Don't lose it. It's just a trick.*

She couldn't look away as the girls' song grew soft and they slowly floated to the ground.

They parted into two columns and as they did, Sam held her breath at the sight of a pale, naked woman on the ground between them. She was staked out, roped at wrists and ankles, completely exposed and helpless. A gag of green cloth invaded her mouth. Long blond hair spilled around her head. Her eyes rolled back in her head. *She sees me!*

One of the robed figures stepped forward, holding a long dagger with a weird wavy blade. It caught the green fire and reflected it. The captive's eyes locked on the weapon.

The high priestess—*that's what she is, she must be some kind of high priestess, what else could she be?*—raised the dagger high, pointed it skyward, and as she did, her robe simply fell off. As if by magic. *Or a button came undone.*

But an instant later, all their robes fell to the ground. *Thirteen,* Sam counted. *There are thirteen of them.* They began their chant once more, and the high priestess, her face made up like an Egyptian queen's, moved forward, stepping between the legs of the captive, lowering herself to her knees.

The blade plunged into the girl's breast. It seemed

to move in slow motion and Sam couldn't look away. The chanting continued as the priestess twisted the weapon. Blood spurted across her painted face, gushed up in a geyser. With an animal cry, the priestess rose, holding the captive's heart up for all to see.

She licked blood from her lips. And then her eyes locked with Sam's.

ABOUT THE AUTHOR

Tamara Thorne lives with her family in California. A full-time writer and part-time ghost hunter, she is the author of six horror novels published by Pinnacle Books: **HAUNTED, MOONFALL, ETERNITY, CANDLE BAY, BAD THINGS,** and **THE FOR-GOTTEN.** Tamara loves hearing from readers. You can send e-mail and sign up for her free newsletter by visiting her Web site at www.tamarathorne.com. You may also write to her c/o Pinnacle Books. Please in-clude a self-addressed stamped postcard if you wish a response.